TOMORROW IS A STRANGER

Although not originally intent on becoming a children's author, Geoffrey Trease, born in 1909, has always loved writing and history, and was able to combine the two in his first children's novel, *Bows Against the Barons*, published in 1934. He is now the celebrated author of some eighty children's books and a number of adult works, including novels and a history of London. His works have appeared in twenty-six countries and twenty languages and many were dramatised as radio serials in the BBC's *Children's Hour*.

Geoffrey Trease has travelled widely in Europe, lived in Russia, and served in India in the Second World War. He now lives in Bath, next door to his daughter, Jocelyn. He also has four granddaughters, twin great-granddaughters and a great-grandson – but, as he says, 'no other pets'!

Geoffrey Trease

Tomorrow is a Stranger

PIPER
PAN MACMILLAN
CHILDREN'S BOOKS

First published in Great Britain 1987 by William Heinemann Ltd

First published in Piper 1989

This Piper edition published 1992 by Pan Macmillan Children's Books
a division of Pan Macmillan Publishers Limited
Cavaye Place London SW10 9PG
and Basingstoke

Associated companies throughout the world

ISBN 0 330 30903 X

1 3 5 7 9 8 6 4 2

A CIP catalogue record for this book is available from
the British Library

Printed in England by Clays Ltd, St Ives plc

Yesterday is safe,
Tomorrow's full of danger,
Yesterday's a face I know,
Tomorrow is a stranger.

ACKNOWLEDGEMENTS

Although all characters in this story are fictitious and bear no resemblance to real persons, a few public figures such as the late Major Sherwill are mentioned by their actual names since they are part of Guernsey history. The book is based closely on the events and conditions of 1940–45 and owes much to eyewitness recollections. The following factual records have been particularly helpful and deserve the author's thanks: *Liberation! The Story of Guernsey in Captivity and the Long Road to Freedom* by Nick Machon, 1985; *Islands in Danger* by Alan Wood and Mary Seaton Wood, 1955; *The Silent War* by Frank Falla, 1967; and *A Child's War* by Molly Bihet, 1985.

The first stanza of Hal Summers' 'A Spell for Midnight' is reprinted from *Tomorrow is My Love: A collection of poems for the young*, © Hal Summers 1978, by kind permission of Oxford University Press.

1

It was fun at first. The gnawing fear came later. It started as an ordinary school day. A golden summer morning. It seemed a shame to be in the classroom.

It was Tessa's week to alter the calendar. She peeled off yesterday's leaf and dropped it into the wastepaper-basket. The new date was one she was to remember all her life.

TUESDAY

18 June

1940

Mr Cooper sat marking the register. Suddenly he muttered, 'Don't know why I'm doing this! What's the point?' He threw down his pencil with a distracted gesture.

Tessa stared. *What's the point?* Of marking the *register* – the sacred register? Was he ill? He looked pale. Perhaps he'd had bad news. He had a son flying with the RAF against the Nazis.

He stood up. She was relieved to see him on his feet, not collapsing or anything. He looked round the class.

'A little less chatter, please! Right, lead on.'

They filed out to Assembly, taking their places as top class at the back of the hall.

Miss Bailey was thumping the piano as usual, Mr Turner mounting the platform, prayerbook in hand. They sang the hymn. George Gasson marched up and read the Lesson. My turn next week, thought Tessa with a nervous pleasure. Mr Turner read the usual prayers and the one he'd added last year when the war broke out . . . 'for all our soldiers and sailors and airmen facing hardship and danger.'

Lately this prayer had become more urgent. At first the war had seemed so uneventful, so boring – only this last month or two had it flared up and become exciting. Hitler had overrun Norway and Denmark, then Holland and Belgium, with his parachutists and panzer columns of tanks. The British forces had made their dramatic escape from the beaches of Dunkirk. Now France was collapsing.

Of course, nothing terrible could happen *here*, Tessa's father had reassured her. 'It'll pass us by as the other war did. The Channel Islands are of no military importance. Hitler won't bother about us.' The only Guernsey people in danger were those who'd gone away to serve, like Mr Cooper's son who was an air-gunner in bombers.

Miss Bailey plonked her way through the final hymn. Mr Turner raised his hand for an announcement. 'I am sorry to tell you, but because of the serious war situation all primary schools are to close for one month from today – '

There was a gasp throughout the hall. A boy near Tessa muttered, 'Hurray!' She sent a dagger-sharp glance along the line. Trust Paul Le Grand to react like that! They'd miss all the end-of-term excitements. Their last term here.

Paul had in fact regretted that instinctive 'hurray' as soon as it had passed his lips. But it wasn't done, in his gang, to admit that you liked school. And in this perfect June weather it was a thrilling thought that the holidays would really be starting now. A pity, though, not to have a proper ceremonial climax. In September he'd be moving up to a different school, bigger, exciting, slightly alarming. He was looking forward to it, but a little wistful as well.

He wouldn't have told his feelings to any one. Meeting Tessa Gray's frown he automatically scowled back. He wasn't going to be corrected by *her*, stupid twit. But no, you couldn't really call the girl stupid. Anything but. Quite bright, often. But irritating, just because she *was* bright – and knew it.

Meanwhile, there'd be these extra weeks of freedom. Bike rides with Ronnie Bush and Bill Hopkins to bays and beaches they'd have to themselves until the holiday crowds came over. But – a new thought – would there *be* a season, would the crowds arrive from England with the war going so badly?

Mr Turner finished his announcement. 'Your parents will be notified as soon as we know anything. Dismiss, then – and God bless you all, wherever you may be.'

They marched out. Bill Hopkins whispered to Paul, 'What's he on about? We'll all still be here.'

'He means next term. The new school and all that.'

Clearing their lockers they all speculated. There was no need for a lot of goodbyes. In such a small island, and a little town like St Peter Port, they were sure to keep seeing each other.

Many were sorry afterwards. But how could they have known that they might never see each other again?

Paul made a date with Bill and Ronnie. Esplanade, usual place, after dinner.

Reaching home, he found the kitchen empty except for Jenny. She stirred, stretched and rose with dignity. She rubbed her dark head affectionately against his leg. He bent and stroked her fur. 'Mum down at the market?' Jenny could not reply, so she lay down again and closed her eyes.

Paul ran upstairs. Gran couldn't get out nowadays. She had the back bedroom so that she could look over the harbour, watching the yachts and fishing-boats, checking if the steamers from Southampton and Weymouth were on time. He had the same view from his attic window overhead, but not so much time to enjoy it. Gran had little else to do when she tired of reading. Though she often said, 'I haven't much time left', she had all the time in the world.

She was glad to see him, but spoke tartly. 'You home? What you been up to?'

'Nothing, Gran. School's closed for a month.'

'It's all holidays for you young people nowadays.'

'It isn't holidays. No one seems to know why it is.'

Gran perked up. She liked a bit of mystery. 'It'll be billets. They'll be sending us a lot more soldiers from England. 'Cause of those Nazis. They'll take over the schools to sleep in.'

He was gazing through the window. 'I can see some soldiers now. Down on the quay.'

'I told you!' Gran loved to be proved right. It seldom

happened so quickly.

'They don't seem to be *landing*,' he said doubtfully. The tiny khaki figures were slowly moving along. 'They're going on board the ship.'

'They're off to France then. To do some fighting, 'stead of hanging about here. That'll be it.'

'But if they're going off to France –' he began to argue.

'They'll send us some more here. That War Office in London! Shifts everybody about without rhyme or reason.'

Mum came home soon after that, basket laden with the week's rations and some fresh fish. 'Best enjoy it while the boats can still go out,' she said. She'd heard about the schools closing. The market buzzed with rumours.

At dinner-time Lucy rushed in, big-eyed and breathless. She only had an hour. She worked at Boots, down the High Street, and she had to come clacking up the steep cobbled side-streets. She'd heard rumours too and was scared. She had a new boy-friend, a soldier from Birmingham. She was meeting him tonight and wondered if he'd be there.

'Your father may know something,' said Mum. But Dad was painting a house on the other side of town.

When Paul got down to the Esplanade he found a ceaseless stream of trucks and hurrying men. As he joined Bill and Ronnie Mr Renouf, the policeman, called to them. 'You lads had best clear off – we're closing this road.'

They obeyed, grumbling. For a while they kicked a ball about in the side-streets, but there was an uneasy, eerie feeling about the day. At tea-time they were ready to go home. Tomorrow, they agreed, they'd take swimsuits and cycle to Belle Greve Bay.

After tea Lucy came in with more rumours. The French had stopped fighting. Our boys were having to get out quick. Just like Dunkirk a few weeks ago. Some were coming out through Cherbourg. The Nazis were hot on their heels.

'Cherbourg?' said Mum. 'Oh, dear, *that's* close!'

Couldn't be much closer, Paul thought. Only about thirty miles across the sea.

Lucy 'dolled herself up', as Gran termed it, and rushed out again. Within the hour she was back, in tears. Her soldier had met her, but only for five minutes. He couldn't stop. He couldn't say why, or when he'd see her again.

Gran was tactful enough to hide her satisfaction. She didn't want Lucy to get mixed up with an Englishman. She should find herself a nice Guernsey boy and stay in the island. Lucy flounced upstairs to her own little attic to take off her glad rags.

Dad came in. He'd heard no news. He'd been up his ladder all day, painting gutters.

'We may know more tomorrow,' said Mum. 'There's a parents' meeting at the school.'

'You'll have to go then. I must get this job finished. Young Alec says he'll work late.' Dad sat back filling his pipe, a big comfortable man, the opposite of Mum who was small and nervy, though pretty as a bird. There was something reassuring about Dad. So calm. A first-class worker, every one said, a craftsman ready to tackle anything.

It had been an odd, worrying day, but Paul slept soundly through the night. The war might be going badly, but so it had done in 1914, Dad said, and of course we'd won in the end.

It was another glorious morning. Paul threw back the black-out curtains and surveyed the harbour, the quays alive with rumbling and clunking, the blue water slashed white by the little boats chugging busily to and fro, the gulls wheeling and screaming. Out there, solid and reassuring, rose the massive huddled ramparts of Castle Cornet at the end of the causeway pointing out to sea like a long granite forefinger. Further out lay the smaller islands, Herm and Jethou and Sark, with France just beyond the horizon.

He wondered what was happening in France. . . .

After breakfast he met Bill and Ronnie, and soon they were skimming away out of town, past North Beach and the gas works, along the gentle curve of the bay.

An RAF plane droned overhead.

'Anson!' cried Bill, who was good at spotting types.

Later, as they sprawled on the hot beach after their swim, a squadron of fighters screeched by. 'Hurricanes,' Bill said. 'They're based on Jersey. Arrived the other day.'

'Good old RAF,' said Ronnie. He gave his famous imitation of an air-gunner downing a Nazi bomber with an ear-splitting burst of fire.

Towards midday they picked up their bikes, dusting off the sand. 'We'll hear what old Turner said at the meeting,' Paul reminded them.

But they did not have to wait until they reached home.

On the Esplanade Vera Lambert flagged them down. Always an excitable girl, Vera was now goggled-eyed. They braked sharply and listened, straddling their bikes.

'Have you heard?' she gasped.

'What?'

'The Germans are coming! We've got to escape – '

'Go on!' said Paul.

'Honest! Mr Turner said so. We've got to be down at the harbour first thing in the morning. One suitcase each.'

2

Vera knew nothing more. One instinct seized the boys: to hurry home. Paul turned into the shadowy lane leading up to his own house. He stood on the pedals, heart pounding, fighting the steep hill.

His mind was racing like his pulse. He remembered cinema newsreels last year. London railway stations, columns of child evacuees, gasmasks slung from shoulders, labels dangling from buttonholes, one suitcase each. . . .

Would *he* be sent off like that – only by ship – to England? Dreadful fears mingled with stupid details. He'd have to leave his stamp album, Mum would fill his case with dull things like vests and pyjamas. . . . But somehow he must slip in his Strictly Private notebook with his secret codes and scribbled poems.

He wheeled thankfully into the level terrace. Dr McNish's car stood outside the house. But he came every week to keep an eye on Gran.

Dad was in the kitchen, conferring with Mum in low urgent tones. They stared at him. 'You've heard then?' said Dad.

'What's happening?' His voice was quivery.

'There's got to be an evacuation,' said Mum.

'But surely the Nazis can't get to us here? The Navy –'

'Even they can't save us this time,' said Dad bitterly. 'I never thought I'd see the day.' His words were like a punch in the stomach. Paul slumped on to a chair.

'I don't see why –'

'Look at your atlas, lad.'

He did not need to. The map was clear enough in his mind's eye. The Channel Islands were much closer to France than to England. Once Hitler held Brittany and the Cherbourg peninsula with bases for his dive-bombers, the seas round Guernsey would be a death-trap for British warships.

'Can't we *all* go?' he pleaded. 'Don't send me by myself. *Please*.'

There was a brisk step on the stairs. The doctor bustled into the kitchen, tall and bald and bony, kindly eyes twinkling.

'What do you think of her?' Mum asked.

The Scotsman pursed his lips. 'Your mother's a wonderful woman, Mrs Le Grand. She's good for a while yet. But I must be frank. She'd not stand the journey.'

'That settles it then,' said Dad.

'Fine,' said Dr McNish approvingly. 'It must be your decision, mind. But don't let the old lady know *why* you're not going.' He looked at Paul. 'You'd not want your Gran worrying that it's for her sake? So – watch your tongue.'

'Yes, doctor.'

Mum asked, awkwardly: 'Shall we see you next week? Some one said you and Mrs McNish would be on the boat tomorrow –'

'And so we shall.' He held up his long finger to check her cry of dismay. 'As you know, my wife's expecting. You'll understand, we want our child born under the Union Jack. So I'm seeing her safe across to Weymouth and her sister will meet her. God willing, I'll be back here on the same boat.'

'You'll come *back*? Even though the Germans –'

'What do you think? *You* won't leave your mother – doctors don't desert their patients. Don't fret, we'll all come through this little bother, never fear.' He patted her shoulder and was gone.

'He's a good man,' said Mum huskily.

Paul gulped. So they weren't going. Any of them. He felt an immense relief. When Lucy came in she agreed at once. Whatever happened, they must stick together.

After dinner Dad hurried back to work. 'Job must be finished,' he said. 'I'll be single-handed now.'

Young Alec must go. Dad had trained him from a boy. but all of military age must get out quick to England. Dad had paid Alec, wished him luck, and told him to be off. Dad would manage somehow.

Paul went to see what his friends were doing. He found the Bush household in turmoil. Suitcases everywhere. The whole family rushing up and down stairs. *They* weren't staying, oh no! Nothing to stay for. Mr Bush was a waiter at one of the big hotels. There'd be no work, no season.

Ronnie couldn't come out. If Paul wasn't going with the school they'd better say goodbye now. Ronnie had to be at the school at five o'clock tomorrow morning. *Five o'clock!*

11

The boys hardly knew what to say to each other. No sense in saying they'd write. Mrs Bush had no idea where they'd be. And if the Nazis invaded Guernsey there'd be no letters passing anyhow.

Shattered, Paul ran round to Bill's. A harassed Mrs Hopkins opened the door. 'No, *we're* not leaving – how can we, with the shop and everything? Of course, we're sending Bill and the girls – we feel it's our duty. I've packed them off to their auntie's to say goodbye. You'll see Bill in the morning, though.' She stopped, seeing his face. 'You are *going*, Paul?'

'No, Mrs Hopkins,' he faltered, 'I'm not.'

'Well, I'm surprised at your parents,' she said disapprovingly. 'Now, I must get on with sorting their things.'

Miserably he wandered down towards the harbour. There were queues outside the shops, people coming away with armfuls of anything that wasn't rationed. Queues even outside the banks, people frantic to draw their money out. The frightened faces frightened *him*. He'd never seen grown-ups looking so scared.

He met several schoolmates. Everybody seemed to be going on the steamer tomorrow. They were surprised that he wasn't.

For once in his life Paul began to wonder if his father was doing the sensible thing. He fought down the disloyal doubt. Of *course* they couldn't leave Gran. His friends hadn't got a gran with a heart condition.

He heard fresh rumours. Some one had come over from Alderney – from there, it was said, a huge black cloud could be seen over Cherbourg, from burning oil stocks that mustn't fall into German hands. Some one else knew a farmer who was shooting his own cows. And a rich old lady had been seen on the quayside, boarding a motor-launch with her maid and chauffeur and all her jewel-cases – she'd got out of her Rolls-Royce and told some man, a complete stranger, that he could have it. 'Better you,' she'd said, 'than the Germans.' Stark panic had seized the island.

Paul turned into one of the dark alleys and clattered down the steps to the waterfront. Bursting out into the sunshine again he ran into Dave Ellis and Johnny Blake wrangling fiercely.

'If your dad's quitting he must be yellow,' Dave was saying.

Johnny answered him with a punch. 'Say that again an' I'll kill you! My dad's under thirty-three. Soon as he gets to England he'll join the army – and *do* something to beat the Nazis, not lie down under 'em!'

Paul saw why he was so indignant. Channel Islanders didn't have conscription. They had their own laws, their own separate governments, the States, and they didn't have to obey the London Parliament in everything though they did have the same king. They could fight for George the Sixth as volunteers, but no one could force them.

He left his classmates arguing and headed for home. Trudging up the lane he saw Tessa Gray come out of her gate. No mistaking that dark-haired leggy figure or that unkempt woolly mongrel she had in tow. When Scamp paused at a lamp-post he could not avoid overtaking her. He had to say something.

'You going tomorrow?'

She gulped. 'Yes.' He saw then that she'd been crying.

'You'll be O.K. Most of the girls in your crowd seem to be going.'

'I know. Are you?'

'No, it's difficult for us.' He explained.

She nodded sympathetically. 'You'll be all right, Paul.'

'Rather,' he agreed. But he didn't feel too sure.

The Gray family, like the Le Grands, would stick together. Only *they* were escaping to England and he felt that Tessa, though her eyes were red now, would enjoy it all as an immense adventure. To see England, the place they were always hearing about! He envied her.

Many parents were having to send their children first and follow later. But Mr Gray thought that they'd get places in the same steamer tomorrow. Bet he's wangled it, thought Paul cynically. Mr Gray had an office job under the States, Public Health Department or something.

'Taking Scamp for a walk?' It was just something to say.

Tessa blurted out, 'Sort of,' and began to sob.

Taken aback, he said another stupid thing. 'Which way?'

'To the *vet's*,' she wailed. 'Where d'you think?'

There was an order: no pets. How could she find a new home for Scamp before tomorrow? With thousands of families in the same awful predicament?

Paul walked beside her, horrified but helpless. He couldn't say, '*We'll* have Scamp for you.' Even if his parents agreed he knew from bitter experience that Jenny would never allow another pet in the house as her rival – least of all a dog. All he could do was keep Tessa company

14

on this tragic last walk.

'And they've let *you* take him?' he said incredulously.

'They didn't let me.' Pride steadied her voice. 'I made them. There's no one else. My father has so much clearing up to do at the office. And Mother's at her wits' end, what with the baby and all the packing and the other two under her feet. I'm the eldest. And Scamp was always specially mine.'

When they got near to the vet's they saw a queue. Everywhere that day there were queues. Dozens of people nursing cats in their arms, leading dogs, or carrying baskets that mewed and spat.

The queue moved very slowly towards the surgery door. Two women in white overalls were taking in the doomed animals. Yet slow as it was, thought Paul, the terror lay really in the smooth, inexorable movement forward. So many pets, all loved by some one, 'put to sleep' as they called it in a mere half-hour of shuffling gradually up to that door.

'What else can you do?' He heard that despairing phrase repeated again and again. No one had an answer.

At last it was their turn. Tessa was paper-white. When she bent suddenly to stroke the dog's head he thought for a ghastly moment that she was going to faint. She didn't, of course. She straightened up and faced the woman at the door.

'Don't worry, dear. He won't know anything. You'd like his collar and lead – '

'I couldn't *bear* it,' said Tessa chokingly and turned away. Paul had to run to catch up with her.

The walk back didn't take so long. 'It *was* good of you,'

15

she said. 'I don't know how I could have gone through with it.' At her gate she said, 'We'd better say goodbye then. We go so early, you won't be awake –'

'I shall! I'll wave to the ship from my window –'

'Oh, *please* do!'

She suddenly thrust her face forward and kissed him. He could never have imagined himself kissing Tessa Gray, of all people, but on this strange dramatic day it seemed the right thing to do. So he did.

'Goodbye, Paul.'

'Goodbye, Tessa. And good luck.'

She ran indoors. He turned away, relieved to see that the lane was empty. No one from school could have seen them. And most likely he and Tessa would never meet again.

3

It had been a long, exhausting day. He slept late and was startled when he drew his black-out curtains and the full glare of the sun struck him.

He remembered his friends. The evacuation! He could see plenty of activity in the harbour, but no sign of the steamer. They must have gone. With a pang of guilt he recalled his promise to wave. Never mind, Tessa wouldn't know. But he did mind.

He pattered down to the bathroom and washed hurriedly. Back in his bedroom, pulling his shirt over his head, he glanced through the window again. A cross-Channel steamer was entering the harbour. So he wasn't too late.

Gobbling his breakfast, he told Mum he was going down to the quay. He must wave goodbye to – to Bill and Ronnie, he hastily corrected himself.

'Well, I'm afraid you can't.'

'Why ever not?'

'Nobody's allowed there unless they're going. Mrs Hobbs had to say goodbye to Daphne at the school.'

Mrs Hobbs had just popped in from next door for a little weep on Mum's shoulder. Mum seemed already to have gathered a whole news bulletin from various neighbours.

'The ships weren't there. Those poor mites were shivering on the quay from six o'clock this morning.'

Paul couldn't quite see Bill and Ronnie as 'poor mites', or even Tessa, for that matter, but he let it pass.

'It's all cordoned off,' his mother said. 'There's troops waiting to embark. We're being left defenceless. They say the fighter planes have gone from Jersey. They'd only *been* there a couple of days.'

Paul had never heard her so bitter. Nobody cared about the Channel Islands! Not a word about them on the BBC!

'Well, Gran won't get upset then,' he reminded her. 'if *we* watch what we say, she won't realise how bad things are.'

Dad came in. 'Ah, there you are, son. I need a hand.'

He was going down to his wholesaler to stock up with paint and other supplies while he could. He wasn't taking the van. Must save petrol now. He'd got out the old hand-cart with Grandpa's name, *Ebenezer Le Grand*, still faintly legible.

They pushed it squeaking and rumbling through the twisty lanes. Dad talked calmly as though business would carry on as usual. 'Houses still have to be painted, specially in this sea air. I expect I'll have my hands full.'

For the moment his order-book was in a mess. Two jobs cancelled: both customers off to England. But another, also getting out, wanted his premises boarded up and made secure. He'd paid cash and gone. Dad was honour-bound to get the work done somehow.

'Things will even out,' he said. 'Awkward, losing Alec, but I'll get by somehow. May find some one else.'

'Wish I could help,' said Paul awkwardly. He'd never wished that before. He knew in his heart he could never take to the work, never make the skilled patient craftsman Dad was.

'You might, son, now and then. But you'll be back at school soon.'

It had hardly occurred to Paul that school might one day open again, even if half the children had gone. Dad said he certainly hoped so. With luck, the Nazis might even not invade the islands, they'd have enough to do attacking the British mainland. Remember what Mr Churchill had said!

Paul remembered all right. The family had sat round the radio, hanging on the Prime Minister's words: 'We shall fight on the beaches, we shall fight on the landing-grounds, we shall fight in the fields and in the streets, we shall fight in the hills. *We shall never surrender.*'

Britain was big enough for that, said Dad. Little islands weren't. They could be pulverised by wave after wave of bombers. No use Guernsey saying, 'never surrender'.

In the end, Dad reckoned, they might be better off than the people who'd crossed to England. *They* might be jumping out of the frying pan into the fire.

They pushed the laden hand-cart back up the hill to the old shed Dad rented as workshop. It smelt pleasantly of wood shavings. Dad was happiest when he had a joinery job: shelves, cupboards, anything he had to measure up and design himself, and then make with loving precision. Paul helped him unload and stack the materials, then went off to see what was happening in the town.

He met several boys from school, but none who were

his particular friends. There was Slippery – Slippery Steve Riley, whose nickname spoke for itself. His grey-green eyes flickered under a jagged fringe of hair cut by his harassed mother when she could lay hold of him. Slippery's grin was amiable but sly. Paul couldn't help admiring the cunning with which he always slid out of trouble at school.

'Hiya, Paul! Have a fag?' Slippery produced a packet.

'No, thanks.'

'Go on, I got plenty! There was this daft old geezer at the little shop last night. In a blind panic he was, thinking the Jerries would be here any minute. Selling off, penny a packet.'

'You mean he served *you*?'

'He wasn't asking for birth certificates! Anyway, I said they were for my dad.'

'You haven't got a dad.'

'He wasn't asking to see dads, either. Come on, be a man.'

Paul shook his head. 'I don't like 'em.' He didn't like that sort of argument either. When he wanted to smoke, he would. But not to kid himself he was a man.

'Please yourself. Take a packet for your dad, then. A bargain. Only threepence to you.'

'He smokes a pipe. And I thought you said a penny?'

'That's what the old geezer was charging. I got to have something for my trouble.'

Copperknob Wilson joined them, his freckled face alive with news. 'Like strawberries?' he asked.

'Don't tell me some one's giving *them* away,' said Paul. 'Penny a basket?'

'Better 'n that,' said Copperknob. 'They're going free.'

'Where?' Slippery's voice was like a whip-crack.

'Not five minutes from here! This old dame was coming out of her front gate. Taxi, piles of luggage. Hurryin' to catch the boat. An' she was hollerin', "Help yourself to anything in the garden! The Germans will if *you* don't." There's strawberries in that garden – '

'What we waiting for?' said Slippery.

Paul went with them. Obviously the lady would never eat the strawberries herself. It was only patriotic to make sure the Germans didn't.

It was a pretty little house, white, with a velvety lawn and two tufted palm-trees. But it looked blank and deserted with its blue shutters barred across the windows.

'Round the back,' muttered Copperknob.

They followed him. A vast strawberry-bed lay before them, starred with white blossoms and fat red berries. They feasted like gluttons. Slippery glanced round. 'There'll be plums in a month or two. And apples. *And* pears.'

Paul thought how fond Gran was of strawberries, how nice it would be to take her a few.

'Good idea,' said Copperknob. 'My mum likes 'em too.'

Slippery had spotted some rows of empty plant-pots ranged under the greenhouse wall. 'Just the thing,' he said. 'Line 'em with a few nice green leaves, fill 'em with strawberries – biggest on top. We could go round selling 'em,' he said wistfully, 'if only we had a barrow.'

Paul hoped they hadn't seen him with his father's hand-cart.

Would it be all right to take a plant-pot? Surely the unknown lady, abandoning her whole home, wouldn't begrudge a pot if it meant a treat for another lady too old and ill to escape? He took one, lined it with fresh greenery, and filled it with the finest berries he could see.

Just then a woman's voice called angrily across the hedge. 'Hi, you boys! What are you up to?'

Copperknob answered, his red face redder than usual. 'Only pickin' some strawberries. The lady said the Germans'd get them – '

'Miss Norrington was saying that to *me* as I helped her into the taxi.' The woman next door peered suspiciously across the trim privet. 'I remember *you*. You were on the pavement, weren't you? All ears!' That was a fair description. After his fiery hair Copperknob's protruding ears were his most conspicuous feature. 'But Miss Norrington wasn't talking to you.'

Knowing Copperknob, Paul guessed that this was true. Embarrassed, he walked over. 'We thought it was all right,' he said, 'we weren't stealing, really we weren't.' He held out the strawberries. 'Would you like to have these?' He could hardly put them back on their stalks.

'No, no,' said the lady, calming down. 'You might as well take them. There *are* so many. Let's say it was a misunderstanding. We've all plenty of bigger things to worry about.'

He thanked her and turned back to his friends. Or, more precisely, to Copperknob. Slippery was nowhere to be seen.

Gran was delighted with the fruit. He did not trouble her

22

with the whole complicated story. He just said, truthfully enough, that they'd been given him by a lady who didn't want them herself.

Looking down from Gran's window he could see no sign of the steamer. So again, he thought, he had failed to keep his promise. Tessa and his other friends must be well on their way to England. He hoped the owner of the strawberries had caught the boat. Anyhow, Dad reckoned there'd be other boats tomorrow. They were trying to get all the school parties away today, but thousands of other people would have to wait a little longer.

Dad thought the steamers would keep up their sailings as long as they could. But with the enemy now on the French coast it would be getting more uncertain day by day, even hour by hour. The time was coming when all the Channel Islands would be cut off from England.

Paul wondered sickly what would happen then. Would the Nazis come over? What would they do to people who'd stayed behind?

He'd followed on the map their terrifying progress in the last month or two. Country after country overrun – Norway, Denmark, Holland, Belgium, and now France. The Nazis held the whole vast arc of Europe's western coasts. Britain, alone unconquered, had the doomed look of a head in a lion's mouth. But not quite so doomed as defenceless little Guernsey.

Dad, puffing his pipe, tried to keep the family calm. What was there here to attract Hitler? Fishing-boats, dairy cows, tomato-houses, not much else. No reason for killing people and wrecking everything.

'They'll maybe send a few soldiers over just to hoist

their flag and all that. If so, we'll just have to keep our heads down while they're here. Can't do much else. But it won't be for ever.'

After dinner Paul wandered disconsolately down the lane. It was better than staying in the house, with its atmosphere of tension. It got you down, the way older people talked over your head, stopped in mid-sentence, caught each other's eyes with warning signals, rephrased their remarks as if you were too young to know the fears that haunted them.

He needed someone of his own age to talk to. But not Slippery Steve again or Copperknob.

He turned the corner. And there was Tessa.

He greeted her with more enthusiasm than he could have imagined possible. 'You've not gone yet! Have you got to wait till tomorrow?'

'We're not going,' she said in a flat voice.

'Not at all? Why ever not?' He saw how dejected she was.

'Father's got to stay. He's essential. That means we all stay.'

She told him how Mr Gray had come home yesterday and broken the news to them. The local government had to go on for the sake of all those who were not being evacuated. The Bailiff and the council members and all the key people under them – it was their duty to remain at their posts.

'Father's Public Health,' Tessa explained. 'If his department closed down there'd be epidemics and food-poisoning.'

Paul saw the truth of that. And if the firemen cleared

out, the police and the ambulance-drivers and people like that, ordinary life would collapse into chaos.

He tried to console her. 'I don't mind all that much,' the girl said, putting a brave face on it. 'Of course, my father could insist on leaving – they couldn't *make* him stay – but he says he must do his duty – '

'He's right, you know.'

'There's just one thing – ' Her voice broke. 'If only we'd known this yesterday, Scamp need never – '

She couldn't go on. He was afraid she was going to burst into tears, but she managed not to.

They went down the hill together in a doleful silence. What could he say? He just gave her bare sunburnt arm the gentlest squeeze, to show that he understood.

4

Tessa soon came to the conclusion that Paul Le Grand was not so bad. Indeed, not bad at all.

At this moment in any case she could not afford to be choosy. Her best friend Beryl was now halfway to England and all the excitements of that fabled land. So were June and Susan. Of the girls in her class who were not being evacuated, none was her particular friend.

Paul must be in a similar predicament. He had always gone around with that Bill Hopkins and Ronnie Bush, but now he was on his own. Nicer, she decided, when away from his gang. Boys often were. Gentler and more sensible. They still had to show off a bit – they were boys, after all – but they weren't so silly with it, not so noisy and aggressive as they were among themselves.

He could have been a whole lot worse, she privately admitted, and he would still have been most welcome in her present time of need. In the past twenty-four hours the bottom had fallen out of her world. Yesterday she had been keyed up by the drama of it all, the adventure of the escape. This morning she had awoken to a world of unbelievable flatness, nothing romantic or new, just the same tidy cramped little bedroom with the childish wallpaper pattern she was tired of, the sentimental pictures she had outgrown.

It was natural that she and Paul should be drawn together during the next few days. There was no school. And he lived just round the corner, up the hill.

'You can see my window,' he told her.

The Le Grands' house stood tall against the sky, part of a terrace. If she poked her head out and counted along the line of upper back windows the seventh was his.

It was harder for him to spot hers because it was sideways on. He had to look down across all the yards and back-gardens. Hers was the tenth house. He'd know it by the great dangling mass of blue clematis.

'Anyhow,' she said, 'I'll hang my towel over the sill when I go in. It's pink this week.'

That gave him an idea. 'We could signal to each other.'

'Only if we were looking out at the same time.'

'No – we could hang out a towel or something. Decide on a code – use different colours. Something to mean, can you come out and meet me? Then something green for "yes" and red for "no".'

It sounded rather complicated, she thought privately, but she didn't want to squash his ideas. He might get huffy.

And, in a way, the very complication of the code had its own attractions. It challenged their ingenuity. They had to think how many different colours they could muster – towels, rugs, dressing-gowns – decide what each colour would stand for, and write out a list each so that there'd be no misunderstandings.

Above all, it was a secret between them. She liked that. The system might be handy when she could not get out.

That was the snag about being a girl. You were useful in the house, so you were nabbed for things at a moment's notice, never mind the upset to your private life. Whatever historic events might be happening, meals had to be laid and washed up, rooms had to be tidied, Shirley's endless nappies strung out on the line – she could have signalled with *them* all right! – and Frank and Harold separated when they fought too fiercely. Her mother couldn't be everywhere at once.

Perhaps all the panic had been for nothing? The Germans hadn't come. The mail boat had resumed service. Beryl had sent her a picture postcard from some village in Devon. Ships were still sailing to England packed with crates of tomatoes. 'Business as usual,' was the motto. Tessa thought of Scamp and wept in the privacy of her room.

This quiet did not last. Father came home from work, slipped thankfully into the thin linen jacket he wore for pottering in the garden, and remarked to her mother, 'There's an open-air meeting tonight. Major Sherwill's going to make a public statement.'

'Oh, Albert! Do you have to go?'

'Certainly not. I shan't hear anything I don't know already.' Father prided himself on always having inside information because of his job with the States.

Major Sherwill was the chief lawyer in the island government, a popular man though English, not Guernsey born and bred. In this crisis he was president of the Controlling Committee.

Tessa was sorry that her father wasn't going to the meeting. She'd never been to a public meeting. She'd have asked him if he'd take her with him.

She had a sudden thought. Why not? She ran upstairs and draped her old green skirt over the windowsill. Paul must have been keeping an eye open. When she went up again ten minutes later she could see the green oblong of his bedside rug. That meant he might be already out and waiting for her in the lane.

It was Tessa who had to wait. As Paul was slipping out through the kitchen door Gran's bell jangled frantically.

'Run and see what she wants,' begged Mum.

Gran was sitting up in bed looking flushed. 'Some great bird went flapping past the window! Nearly gave me one of my turns!'

He flung up the sash and leant out. 'It wasn't a bird, Gran. It was my rug – I can see it down in the yard.'

'Why should your rug get up off the floor and fly?'

'It didn't.' By now his face was as flushed as Gran's. 'I'd hung it out. To – er – air.'

'Well, it startled me! Might have been that Dracula!'

'Sorry, Gran.'

He rushed downstairs, retrieved the rug, took it back to his room, and escaped at last to meet Tessa.

She told him about the meeting. It was to be in the main street, down by the church. They'd plenty of time. Hour and a half yet. He agreed at once.

It was another beautiful evening, the air soft as velvet, the harbour glassy, Castle Cornet golden in the sloping sun. There was a queue of lorries along the quay with crates of tomatoes for the English markets. The *Isle of Sark* was loading them. Another steamer was disembarking cattle and horses from Alderney.

Cutting through into the High Street, Paul and Tessa joined the gathering crowd. By the time Major Sherwill appeared there were hundreds of people.

He looked what Mrs Gray always called him, 'a proper gentleman', tall and good-looking. He had a fine record from the first war, wounded in nine places, awarded the Military Cross for courage under fire. A good man to put in charge at a time like this.

His speech was very simple, cheerful, even humorous. That reassured everybody. After all, *he* was staying in Guernsey although he was English. So was his popular wife, with their young children. If *they* thought it was all right –

'What's "demilitarised"?' Paul whispered.

Thanks to her father, Tessa knew. 'It means we're not trying to defend the islands,' she answered hoarsely. 'Wouldn't be any good. That's why the soldiers left.'

The Major explained that they couldn't possibly beat the Germans if they did come and it would be suicide to try. A voice or two cried 'Shame!' but most people obviously agreed with the Major. You couldn't say that *he* was a coward.

The meeting ended. Paul and Tessa turned homewards up the High Street. It was at that moment that the war – for them – began in earnest.

It was just like the films.

Out of the placid evening sky the planes came screeching down over housetops and harbour. Machine-guns rattled. Streams of bullets drew splintered lines across walls. Windows shattered into sprays of murderous fragments.

A scream of terror died on Tessa's lips as Paul grabbed her, hurling them both into an alley. They nearly fell down the shadowy steps that led to the quayside. Instead, they clung to each other under the archway.

They could hear footsteps running in panic along the street, shouted orders, cries and moans. Then the planes swept back, low, deafeningly low, guns blazing. From a distance came the crump of bombs, the delayed crash of a collapsing building, the slow slide of chinking rubble like shingle on the beach.

'How are we going to get *home*?' she wailed.

Paul was wondering too. Later he admitted to her that he'd kept saying to himself, 'Mum will be so *mad* if I'm stupid and get killed.' Funny, really. But not at the time. Not funny at all.

Again that fiendish roar of swooping aircraft. Again the rat-ta-tat of machine-guns, the whine and thump of bombs. They'd be mad to risk the High Street. It stretched through the town-centre, a conspicuous guide-line for low-flying pilots. The Nazis could *fillet* St Peter Port, taking it out like the backbone of a fish.

Somehow, though, they must get home. Their parents would be worried sick. Also – the ghastly realisation dawned on him – the raid wasn't happening only here. All the more reason to get home and make sure that everybody there was all right.

'Better go down here,' he grunted.

They turned from the death-trap of the High Street and went down the dank stone steps. But coming out into the evening brightness of the waterfront they saw that they

31

had exchanged the frying-pan for the fire.

Quite literally fire. Manes of crackling orange flame, flaring skywards into clouds of stinking grey smoke.

The very road was ablaze. The raiders had traversed the line of stationary lorries, pumping bullets into them at close range. Petrol had gushed from the perforated fuel-tanks, washed across the road and exploded into flame.

Amid this inferno figures staggered, fell, writhed in agony. Some had been caught where they huddled in their cabs. Others, diving for shelter under their trucks, had met the deadly spray of the escaping petrol and were now themselves alight.

The harbourside warehouses were built over arcaded passageways. Paul seized Tessa's hand and raced her along under this partial protection. Then a new horror met their eyes. It seemed that the roadway was a mass of blood and – an unthinkable pulp, wet and vivid red.

Tessa let out a choking laugh. 'It's only tomatoes!'

So it was, mostly. A bomb had exploded amid hundreds of crates of the ripe produce.

They ran on, lungs bursting, into another scene of chaos. The farm animals just landed from Alderney had stampeded at the gunfire. They were plunging and rearing madly all over the road. There was a new danger, of getting kicked or gored or crushed against a wall. 'Up here!' he yelled, and hustled her up a side-turning back into the town.

It was quieter there now. They could make for home, zig-zagging through the byways. Glancing back over the rooftops they could see a vast pall of smoke rolling up from the harbour.

Both were welcomed with immense relief when they arrived – and their own relief was no less to find their houses intact and their families unharmed.

Tessa's father, at the first alarm, had seized steel helmet and gasmask and rushed off to his post. It was midnight when he returned, but Tessa was still downstairs. Who could go to bed on such a night? She heard him say wearily, as her mother made yet another pot of tea: 'Twenty fatal casualties, Milly – so far. It'll be more when we get the full list.'

Paul found even Gran downstairs, where she hadn't been for ages. Dad had insisted. No one, he said firmly, was going to stay upstairs tonight. They'd made up a bed for her in the living-room. She was rather enjoying being at the centre of life again.

They switched on the BBC News. Not a word about the raid – *their* raid. Only an official announcement that the Channel Islands had been declared 'open cities'.

'Cities?' said Gran. 'We're not cities.'

'It's just the word they use,' Dad explained patiently. 'Usually it *is* for cities – like Paris the other day. The point is, they're not being defended, they're not military objectives, so there's no excuse for bombing them.'

'H'm,' said Gran disgustedly. 'They might have mentioned that to Hitler a bit sooner.'

5

After such a night every one was jaded and nervous. Reaction set in. The morning sunshine seemed a mockery.

Knowing now what had happened down at the harbour, Mrs Gray was shaken by Tessa's narrow escape.

She could not grasp that Tessa had only partially registered the horror. She had been terrified, yes, but it had all been mercifully quick. Racing for home, half-blinded by the acrid smoke, she had been only vaguely aware of other people. Not until today had she learned gradually of all the tragic deaths, the frightful injuries.

Tessa was relieved that she was not scolded for being there at all. Her parents were too thankful to have her back unharmed. Her father did ask, 'Who were you with?' She could answer truthfully enough that lots of people from school had been at the meeting. 'Paul Le Grand saw me home,' she said casually. 'He lives just up the hill.'

'I know,' said her mother. Of course. In St Peter Port everybody knew where everybody else lived.

Her mother wouldn't let her father ask any more questions. 'The girl's still in a state of shock. Awful sights for a child to witness!' She put her arm round Tessa. 'Try to forget it, darling. You're safe now, thank God.'

Tessa did not intend to forget anything. She was only vexed that she could not remember more. It had been the most exciting adventure in her life so far. She must write to Beryl with every dramatic detail.

She was glad that she'd been able to mention Paul to her parents. It removed a slight awkwardness that had been on her conscience. She hadn't been *hiding* anything. She just hadn't referred to their being friends. It would be easier in future.

Paul gave a very similar account of last night's events, also dropping Tessa's name.

'You did right, son, to see her home,' said Dad.

'It was gentlemanly,' said Gran approvingly.

Later, Mum met Mrs Gray down at the shops. Mrs Gray asked after Paul and sent her thanks for making sure that Tessa got home safely.

The town, needless to say, had been seething with sensational rumours. Later Paul was able to get the facts from Tessa. All the casualty reports had gone through her father's office, and though he was always very fussy about keeping 'official secrets' he knew that the Controlling Committee was anxious to scotch the wilder stories.

No, he'd said, there hadn't been fifty people killed. The doctors and Civil Defence had reported twenty-nine so far. That was bad enough, for Heaven's sake. It was true that the Nazis had machine-gunned an ambulance – one of the casualties had been killed and an ambulance-man badly wounded. It was true that one plane had dived on the lifeboat which happened to be out at sea, and though it was clearly marked as a lifeboat it had been riddled with bullets, and the coxswain's son killed.

Everyone was dreading another raid. 'We all sleep downstairs tonight,' said Mr Le Grand. 'And tomorrow, Sunday or not, I'll start building a proper shelter.'

But he only started. Because it was the very next day that the Germans arrived.

Paul had often wondered in his more anxious moods just how they would come, if they ever did.

He remembered cinema news reels. Common sense told him that there couldn't be thousands of tanks like those that had swept suddenly over the plains of Poland. Would the enemy come ashore in some lonely cove and burst into the town waving swastika flags and shouting 'Heil Hitler'? Or, as the harbour was undefended, would their ships sail boldly in and disgorge hordes of grey-green figures blazing away at everything that moved? Or would it be like Norway – a mighty droning of troop-carrying planes and then the whole sky flowering with a thousand parachutes?

'Well, they won't come by taxi, that's for sure,' said Slippery contemptuously when Paul met him in the street that Sunday morning.

Slippery, being a choirboy, was on his way to church. He glanced at his new wristwatch. He had found it first thing yesterday, when he went out very early to inspect the air-raid damage before the mess was cleared and the shop-windows boarded up. 'Can't stop now,' he said. The church he attended was on the far side of town, but it ran quite the best outings.

For once Slippery was mistaken. Come by taxi was precisely what some of the Germans did.

Later in the day Paul and Tessa were sunning themselves on the sea-wall opposite the big hotel, the Royal.

Suddenly up swept a little procession of police cars, followed by a taxi. They drew up in front of the hotel. Paul and Tessa ran across. A small crowd had appeared from nowhere.

Policemen were getting out. But there were other uniforms Paul had never seen in real life – only in films. The Luftwaffe! 'They've caught some parachutists,' he told Tessa. Then the triumph faded from his voice.

These German officers did not look like crestfallen captives. They positively swaggered up the steps into the hotel. One German stayed outside, holding a gun. The Guernsey policemen stood around on the pavement, looking sheepish, declining to answer people's questions.

Only the taxi-driver seemed eager to talk. He'd been called to the airport urgently, he said, because the police hadn't enough cars. 'Wasn't my idea,' he declared emphatically. 'If it was left to me I wouldn't let any of these blighters inside my cab.'

'Watch your tongue, Sam,' a constable muttered.

But Sam was enjoying his rapt audience. 'Seems they'd just come down on the airfield. Nothing to stop 'em, barring a few cows. Inspector Sculpher was there with a letter to hand to them, polite as you like. No armed forces here, so no resistance.'

The taximan's tone was withering. An elderly man broke in, protesting. 'He was only obeying instructions. There mustn't be any resistance, or there'll be most appalling bloodshed.'

This brought murmurs of agreement, so the driver

changed his tack. 'There's thirty thousand gallons of aviation spirit up at the airport. Now the Jerries have got the lot!'

'Don't worry, Sam,' said a new voice, 'it won't be much use to them. The RAF boys saw to that before they left. They put sugar in those storage-tanks, and sand, and tar. . . . You name it.'

Laughter rippled round the crowd. Then a hush fell as another car drew up. A Luftwaffe officer got out, and a tight-lipped Major Sherwill. They entered the hotel.

Time passed. Nothing more happened. Tessa and Paul decided to go home and spread the news.

As they turned the corner, deep in excited talk, Paul had the narrowest escape. A motor-cyclist thundered past, missing him by inches.

'Did you see *that*?' he gasped, clutching Tessa's arm. 'What's he playing at? Wrong side of the road and – '

'It was a German. A German soldier!'

Suddenly the full significance of the new situation was brought home to them. The motor-cyclist hadn't been on the wrong side from *his* point of view. It was the right side, the proper side – in Germany. From now on they were, in a sense, *in* Germany. They'd have to get used to it.

Tessa went cold. Until now she'd been living in the familiar reassuring world she had known since she was born. Even the horrifying events of Friday evening had not really altered that.

Now everything – *everything* – was going to be different, uncertain, filled with fear of the unknown.

Her mother had a stock saying in times of stress: 'Well,

we'll just have to see what tomorrow will bring.'

What else could you do? Tomorrow always came. You couldn't stop it. But Tessa was wondering now how she could face tomorrow.

It would be like opening the door to a frightening stranger. Perhaps, as in some paralysing nightmare, opening the door to a man with only a skull beneath his hat. A faceless stranger.

6

To Paul, tomorrow came early. The insistent unending drone of aircraft woke him long before his usual hour.

An air raid! He hadn't heard a siren. He jumped out of bed. He must rouse the others –

Then he remembered. The Germans were here already. They wouldn't bomb themselves.

He threw back the black-out curtains, screwing up his eyes against the brightness. More planes were rumbling overhead. From the sound he wondered if they were troop-carriers.

He opened his door cautiously. He did not want to disturb the family. No sound from below. But he was thankful that Jenny instantly materialised from nowhere, nuzzled his pyjama leg, and leapt silently on to his bed. It was not a moment to be entirely alone.

He pulled on his clothes. Washing could wait. He picked up a book but could not get interested. He remembered his *Schoolboy's Diary*, given him by Lucy last Christmas. He'd never kept it regularly. This seemed the time to start.

Against *Sunday 30 June* he wrote: '*The Germans arrived.*' Against *Friday* he recorded the air raid and the casualty figures. He sat with pen poised over the blank space for *Monday*. He wondered uneasily what would happen today.

There wasn't room for a lengthy chronicle. The diary allowed only one double-page spread for each week. The rest was printed information – First Aid, sports records, famous anniversaries. Some bits were more useless than others. Not many boys needed the Greek alphabet. Though actually, when he'd been in a secret gang with Bill and Ronnie, he'd tried to persuade them to adopt it for coded messages. They'd given it up as boring, but he could still spell out English words in the strange beautiful lettering the ancient Greeks had used.

Now he had found a use for this knowledge at last! He'd hesitated about writing *Tessa and I*. Some one might pick up his diary and make fun of him. But if he turned each letter into its Greek equivalent . . . *Tessa and I ran home under enemy fire*, he wrote slowly and carefully.

After this mental effort he played with Jenny for a few minutes. 'And *you* won't forget the raid, will you?' he whispered into her fur. The explosions had scared her. She'd shot out of the house like a rocket, Dad said. They didn't see her again until the next morning.

By now bathroom and kitchen noises were drifting upstairs. He smelt frizzling bacon. It seemed a good moment to go down.

After breakfast he ran off to fetch the paper. There'd been no London newspapers yesterday, and there weren't likely to be today. But Gran would expect her *Guernsey Star*. She'd never been out of the islands and it was the local news that mattered to her. She could get enough of the world's wickedness, she always said, from the BBC.

Despite the arrival of the invaders the paper had been published. The headlines were black and heavy.

ORDERS OF THE COMMANDANT
OF THE GERMAN FORCES
IN OCCUPATION OF THE
ISLAND OF GUERNSEY

He stood on the pavement, goggling at the proclamation.

(1) All inhabitants must be indoors by 11 pm and must not leave their homes before 6 am.

(2) We will respect the population in Guernsey; but, should anyone attempt to cause the least trouble, serious measures will be taken and the town will be bombed.

There were eleven regulations altogether. Weapons must all be handed in, even old souvenirs. The black-out was to be observed as before. Private use of cars was banned. The list was signed: *The German Commandant of the island of Guernsey, July 1, 1940.*

'Please?' said a deep voice.

Paul lowered the newspaper. Slowly his startled eyes travelled upwards from the immense jackboots, up the green breeches and tunic, with its belt and straps and dangling hand-grenades, to the bronzed face smiling down from under the basin-shaped helmet.

'Good – morning,' went on the soldier, carefully, as if the English language might break under him.

'Good morning,' said Paul mechanically.

'Please – how far – is London?'

'I don't know.' If he had known he wouldn't have said.

'This is – England? *Ja*?'

'No, it's Guernsey.'

The soldier looked as if he had never heard of the island. He said, confidently, 'We go – now – to London!'

An imp of mischief prompted Paul to say, 'Then you'd best take those boots off, or you'll get them very wet!' He was scared when he'd said it, but obviously the man hadn't understood. 'Thank you. Good boy,' he said benevolently, and sauntered away.

Paul could have hugged himself. He'd spoken to a German, he'd made fun of him – and got away with it. Wait till he told everybody! But his exultation quickly faded as he walked home. A red-white-and-black swastika flag was flapping over the Royal Hotel. There was a stony-faced sentry outside. Paul wouldn't have tried to pull *his* leg.

Dad glanced at Gran's paper before it went upstairs.

'Doesn't look too bad. So far.' But he snorted when he saw that airguns were included with the 'pistols, revolvers, daggers' that must be handed in at the hotel by midday. His own boyhood airgun had been promised to Paul.

'They'd never know,' he grunted.

'*You* never know! Hand it in,' Mum begged, nervously. Lucy too was looking very white. The proclamation said that the shops must open as usual. Mum gave her a shrewd glance and then caught Paul's eye. 'You might walk your sister down to work. Something for you to do.' Lucy looked relieved.

When they got near the High Street they saw the grey green uniforms everywhere. A long column came tramping up from the Esplanade, band blaring, rank after rank of bobbing helmets and swinging arms. Other soldiers in ones and twos strolled along the pavements, still in battle order with rifles and hand-grenades, exclaiming at the goods in the shop-windows.

When Lucy came home she said the counters had been besieged. The Germans were buying up everything, to send to their families.

'They'd only their own money,' she said. 'We didn't know what to do. But the manager said we must take their German marks. That's the money now. One mark is two shillings.'

'Scandalous!' said Gran, who hadn't been shopping for years. Mum said at least it was better than looting.

When Paul met Tessa she had calmed down since the day before. 'Father says the Germans are very anxious to be "correct". It's their favourite word. Some of them hardly know where they are.'

He told her of the soldier he'd warned about getting his feet wet. 'You *never*!' she cried. Her admiration warmed him.

Major Sherwill's committee had to pass on instructions from the German military headquarters. 'We mustn't sing *God Save the King*,' she said.

They could still listen to the National Anthem on the BBC. Paul's father would turn up the volume so that it resounded through the open window. The news bulletins were full of Britain's preparations against her own invasion. Tank traps and minefields everywhere.... All fit civilians enrolling as Local Defence Volunteers...

'If the Jerries set foot in England,' said Dad, 'they'll

find it a sight different from Guernsey!'

Tessa's father could not show such defiance. The office instructions were to behave as 'correctly' as the Germans.

'It seems they never wanted a war with Britain,' Mr Gray explained to the family. 'Hitler admires Britain. He thinks we ought to be friends.'

Hitler hoped that the British would now admit that they had lost. If Churchill wouldn't accept that, they must get rid of him. Meanwhile the Channel Islands were to be treated gently.

Certainly, in that first week, the invaders made a good impression. They seldom got drunk. They did not annoy the local girls. They seemed homesick. They showed photos of their families. They liked children and gave them sweets. Frank and Harold got some. Then a rumour started that the sweets were poisoned.

Tessa was doubtfully studying a bar of chocolate when Slippery came along the street. He exclaimed in horror. 'You're never going to eat that?'

'Well. . . .'

'It's *your* life. If you choose to take the risk –'

That put her off completely. 'I'll chuck it away.'

'In that case – ' He plucked it from her fingers.

'*You're* not going to eat it?'

'What you take me for? I'll . . . dispose of it.'

He saw Paul coming and made a quick departure. 'You are a chump,' Paul told Tessa. 'He's selling them.'

'But people do say that the Germans –'

'Maybe. But how could this bar be poisoned? I bet it was bought here in the High Street.'

Tessa checked with her father. The Public Health office

had found no poisoned sweets. It never did.

July continued fine. It was a shame that there were no holiday visitors. The German bands gave concerts in the open air, lively waltzes and polkas as well as marches. Tessa felt guilty as her feet moved to the rhythm – she shouldn't be enjoying the music, but it did bring some colour and gaiety into the depressing greyness of wartime. But besides providing music the invaders were mining the beaches and unrolling miles of barbed wire along the cliffs. Most bathing places and picnic spots were out of bounds.

She and Paul had given up their signalling system as too dangerous. Her father had been horrified to look up from his gardening and see two towels suspended from her window. He had barely listened to her feeble explanation. 'Don't you realise,' he said, 'the Germans might think you were *signalling*? Perhaps to a British submarine! We should all be in terrible trouble.'

So they had to abandon that idea. They managed to meet without it.

One day they arranged with George Gasson to cycle over to his uncle's farm on the west coast. Rounding a bend they almost ran into a couple of German soldiers.

A barked order made them brake sharply. They found themselves staring into two rifle-muzzles. Seeing how young they were the soldiers lowered their weapons.

'*Verboten*!' shouted one, and let out a stream of German.

They turned their machines, prepared for a long detour, but the other soldier called them back. He held out his hands side by side. '*Nein!*' he said emphatically. Then he extended one hand ahead of the other. '*Ja!*' he said and smiled.

'I get it,' George cried. 'Mustn't ride two or three abreast. Single file only.'

There was a regulation but they had all forgotten it. The less agreeable German held out *his* hand, but palm uppermost. '*Eine mark, bitte.*'

They groped in their pockets, trying to muster two shillings. But the other soldier said something to his comrade and waved them on. After that they took care to observe the new rule.

Every day the cloudless sky pulsed with aircraft: no longer just troop-carriers and transports. The Luftwaffe had established a fighter base.

George was a keen spotter. 'The bombers come over from France,' he explained, 'and circle the airfield before flying on to raid England. The fighters here take off to escort them. Fighters can't carry so much fuel, so it shortens the distance for them.'

It was a sad thought that Guernsey was so useful to the enemy. But before long the RAF struck back. On 9 August Paul could make a gleeful entry in his diary: '*RAF bombed airfield.*' Nobody knew if any German fighters had been caught on the ground or what damage had been done to the runway.

The holidays had lasted so long. They talked wistfully of school, wondering what would happen. Mrs Gray hoped desperately that there would be something to take the boys off her hands.

'Don't worry,' her husband assured her. 'Something will be arranged.'

He had to admit that, although Public Health had its problems, his colleagues in Education were running about like demented ants, though he would not have put it like that to any one outside his own family. With his inborn respect for local government Mr Gray always spoke about mergers, temporary expedients and necessary compromises. He was very fond of phrases like *pro tem* and *ad hoc*.

Tessa was quite wily in gradually wheedling information out of him. 'Don't worry,' he said again. 'Just between ourselves, I went into Education today about a quite different matter – and I just *happened* to see a list with your name on it. They're organizing a new school. You'll be going into it all right.'

'Oh, *good*!' She couldn't help asking, 'Did you see who else?'

He hesitated. 'Well . . . let me see. The Gasson boy. He was next to you in the alphabetical order.'

She longed to ask about Paul but daren't.

It was all right, though. When the parents got their notifications Paul learnt that he was going to the same school.

7

It felt strange after being top dogs to be lowly first-years again.

Some of the boys and girls streaming into the playground were immense. Some had cycled from the far ends of the island. Even familiar faces looked different – like Tessa's, smiling nervously above the neat tie and and gym-slip of her uniform.

There were only about a hundred altogether. The staff had been gathered from various sources. The tweed-suited lady with short grey hair, sitting very erect at the piano, was Miss Grimbly, a well-known local character. Paul's father had done work on her cliff-top cottage above the town.

At Assembly the headmaster, Mr Dexter, spoke of the difficult times they lived in. He sounded ill at ease, choosing his words as though afraid of offending the Germans. When he dismissed them Miss Grimbly broke into a popular tune on the piano. At his agitated signal she broke off.

'Miss Grimbly! Is that entirely – appropriate?'

'Entirely, Headmaster.'

'Oh – well . . .' he said weakly.

With a toss of her head Miss Grimbly resumed her

rendering of *There'll always be an England*.

They met her again after break. 'I am Music,' she announced, facing the class with a no-nonsense expression, 'but it appears that I am also expected to teach you History. I shall do my best. Do not be surprised if I constantly have to look things up myself. Looking things up – unashamedly – is the beginning of scholarship. I shall not trouble you much with dates. Arabs, I am told, can live almost indefinitely on dates. We are not Arabs.'

There were some giggles. She quelled them. She wrote down their names. 'Your father is Mr Joe Le Grand?' she asked Paul. 'I hope you are half as good a worker!' He blushed, but liked the compliment to Dad.

The worst shock that first day was the news that every child was now to learn German – by order of the Commandant.

Grumbling rebelliously they filed into the first lesson. It was some consolation to find that they were to be taught by the youngest and quite the prettiest member of the staff. Miss Goldsmith was fair-haired and slim with a welcoming smile and a vivacious manner. She had a slight accent.

'No,' she said at once, 'I am *not* German. Perhaps we should clear that point! I come from Austria, where also we speak German. It was a separate state until two years ago, when it was . . . joined . . . to the German Reich.' Her voice wavered. 'Since that time I have been in Britain.' She shut her lips tightly. Every one knew what she meant.

Lessons with her proved far more enjoyable than anyone had expected. She taught them songs and games, showed them pictures of her home city, Salzburg, and the lakes and forests and snow-crusted peaks of her country. Without noticing it, they picked up German words and phrases. German was not just the enemy's language, it was Miss Goldsmith's too.

The boys were harder to win over than the girls. They liked Miss Goldsmith – she soon became 'Goldilocks' – but they did not like learning any foreign language, getting their tongues round peculiar syllables, feeling silly when they got things wrong. The girls took to it more easily. They could laugh at themselves. Tessa in particular would always have a go.

Goldilocks teased the boys. 'You Englishmen are all the same!' (They liked the 'men' part.) 'You are so self-conscious. If you cannot speak perfectly you remain silent. Do you play your cricket so? If you cannot make a hundred runs do you refuse to play at all?'

Some thought it unpatriotic to learn a language forced upon them. Others said, 'What's the use? The Jerries won't be here for ever. One day they'll be kicked out.' Paul was less optimistic. Suppose they did stay for ever?

But no, the British would win the war. The world would be free again. He'd be grown up, he'd travel, perhaps he'd climb those mountains, sit in those open-air cafés she told them about, drinking the 'white' wine that was really more the colour of liquid gold. Some sense then in knowing the lingo.

Or suppose – and now his romantic imagination took off in earnest – just suppose one day he had to escape from a Nazi prison. Cross Germany in disguise. Useful to speak German like a native!

Copperknob Wilson was among those who remained

stubbornly opposed to the lessons, and with some reason, for he could not spell English let alone the long German words Miss Goldsmith wrote on the board. Slippery pretended he could have learnt if he'd wanted to. He had his own excuse for resisting her charm.

'Course she's a good looker! So what? Never heard of a beautiful spy?'

'Goldilocks?' said George. 'Don't be daft.'

Tessa said, 'Why should they want a spy in our school?'

'They want to know what people are saying. Kids pass on things they hear at home. Who is she, anyway?' Slippery demanded. 'No one's ever seen her before. Where's she come from?'

'Austria,' said Paul. 'She told us. Not Germany.'

'Same thing.' Slippery had never been good at Geography. He could not turn them against her, but he managed to create a faintly suspicious atmosphere.

September turned into October. The BBC reported mass raids on London, terrible fires and devastation. Hitler's air chief, Goering, was trying to bomb Britain into surrender.

There were raids on Guernsey too – by the RAF. In the middle of the night the sirens went and the German batteries barked and banged. Unless the RAF could identify a military target they mostly dropped leaflets and British newspapers. There was a heavy penalty for possessing them. You had to hand them in to the police. Few people did. Some were passed round in school, and the teachers pretended not to notice.

One evening Paul went to the cinema with his parents.

It was *The Barretts of Wimpole Street* yet again. The occupation had cut off the supply of films, so that the few that had been in Guernsey on that fateful week-end had to be run and re-run, along with foreign pictures subtitled in English. German troops sat on one side, local people on the other, divided by a heavy iron rail down the gangway.

The newsreel was naturally from the Nazi point of view. Hitler strutting in triumph through the Europe he had conquered ... swastika banners tossing... arms slanting in salute... hysterical crowds chanting '*Sieg heil!*'

And the Luftwaffe flying over London, raining down bombs into the smoke pall beneath.... No mention of planes failing to return. According to the newsreel the RAF was destroyed as a fighting force, the Royal Family were to take refuge in Canada. So was Churchill –

This was too much for Paul's father. His disbelieving laugh rang through the cinema. Other people joined in, and began to clap sarcastically.

The lights came on. Two purple-faced German policemen appeared at the end of the row. 'They want *you*, Dad,' Paul whispered in panic. He imagined his father dragged away to prison, perhaps deported to Germany. It proved less serious. The policemen pointed angrily to the notices on the wall. IT IS STRICTLY FORBIDDEN TO APPLAUD. The Nazis had found that people always clapped in the wrong places.

Mr Le Grand had to pay a spot-fine of ten marks. He said afterwards that it had been worth every penny. Paul's mother, however, was greatly upset. It was a long time before she let Dad take her to the cinema again.

In November the Germans confiscated all wireless sets for six weeks. They were constantly making new regulations as they settled in. There was no more talk of invading England, but they were certainly staying in Guernsey.

Island law was being brought into line with German. Like it or not, the States had to adopt whatever the Commandant laid before them. 'They've no choice,' Mr Gray explained. 'We're a conquered country. Our government can't be anything but a rubber stamp.'

Even he was rebellious when the States had to pass the anti-Jewish laws of Germany. No Jew could be a citizen; marriage with a Jew was illegal.

'But *are* there any Jews in Guernsey?' asked Mrs Gray.

'It's the principle, Milly! This is a wicked, immoral law. I'm ashamed it's been voted on to our statute-book.'

There was much more indignation in the town over the banning of the Salvation Army. Because it used the word 'army' and wore uniform the Germans seemed to imagine it was a military organization that could be used against them.

Despite everything, Miss Goldsmith's lessons remained popular, always interesting, occasionally hilarious.

One day she was teaching them the numerals. A boy and girl came out in front and pretended to order a meal in a restaurant. Another boy acted the waiter, calling out the prices. Everyone scribbled down what the bill should be. Hardly any two people got the same total. They were all in hysterics when the headmaster walked in, followed by a tall young officer.

The laughter died, Miss Goldsmith's smile faded. Mr Dexter introduced the officer who clicked his heels, bowed to Miss Goldsmith, and repeated, 'Oberleutnant Fischer'. Mr Dexter stared in a bemused way at the boy playing the waiter with the blackboard duster draped over his arm.

Miss Goldsmith sent the actors back to their seats and explained her method. 'Then I – I'll leave you to it,' said Mr Dexter and fled, thankfully. The officer nodded to Miss Goldsmith and she turned to the class.

'Oberleutnant Fischer has come to see how you are getting on. Do not be afraid. Stand up when you are asked a question, and speak up. Now we shall speak only German.'

The oberleutnant was not at all alarming. He did not bark at them but spoke slowly and made his questions simple. 'We shall continue with the numerals. You know the names of the months? I will ask you your birthdays.'

You had time to prepare. So long as you did not come out with an impossible date like the thirtieth of February the officer could not fault you. Even the dim Copperknob was eventually coaxed into an acceptable answer.

Oberleutnant Fischer seemed pleased with their progress. He asked a few general questions that were not so easy to answer in German.

'When did England first conquer Guernsey?' Tessa put up her hand. 'Yes?' he said.

Slowly and carefully she framed the answer. 'Please, Herr Oberleutnant, England never conquered Guernsey. *We* conquered England. Under our ruler, the Duke of

Normandy. In . . . er . . . one thousand and sixty-six.'

'So?' His jaw dropped.

Miss Goldilocks could hardly hide her smile. 'It is so, Herr Oberleutnant. It was William the Conqueror. He became King of England.'

'That is most interesting.' He looked as though it really was.

Even Slippery muttered in grudging admiration, 'She fixed him proper, that time.'

The officer picked up his gloves and cane. 'Goodbye, children. I shall come again to see you and discover what progress you have made. So work hard.' He chuckled. 'You will never know when to expect me.'

He bowed to Goldilocks, saluted and went.

'See the look he gave her?' George whispered to Paul.

'What sort of look?'

'Hard to explain. But – it was funny, somehow.'

Miss Goldsmith had rather a funny look herself. Being inspected must be a strain even for teachers.

8

Nobody could imagine what Christmas would be like. Of course the Germans *had* Christmas. Miss Goldsmith taught the class a German carol.

Oberleutnant Fischer found them learning the words when he dropped in for another inspection. He gave Miss Goldsmith another of his curious glances.

'So! You teach them our carols.'

'Yes, it is a good way to learn the language.'

'I agree, Fräulein Goldsmith. I – but never mind – '

When he had tested them he relaxed and described in his fluent English how he and his young family kept Christmas at home in Heidelberg.

A pity, thought Tessa, that all Germans weren't like him. The occupation had two faces, one friendly, the other harsh. One day Paul had just returned from school when there was a tremendous banging on the front door. An immense sergeant-major stood there, clipboard and pencil in hand.

'Le Grand?' he barked.

'Ja – Herr – er – ' Paul floundered.

'Ask him what he wants,' Mum called from the kitchen. Mum thought that if you had German lessons at school you knew the whole language.

Luckily for Paul the sergeant-major stood aside with a great stamping of feet and an elderly officer with spectacles walked into the house. He greeted Mum in halting English. All houses were to be inspected as possible billets.

'I've dreaded this,' she moaned.

He asked the size of the family and the number of rooms. The sergeant-major scribbled. They saw the kitchen and the outside lavatory, then marched upstairs. Paul trotted behind to give Mum moral support.

He was in despair. They'd be sure to billet soldiers here. Most likely they'd take over the whole house. Other families had been turned out of their homes.

'They can't go into Gran's room,' said Mum, flustered. But the sergeant-major flung open the door. There was something like a squawk of outrage from within.

Gran was sitting by the window in her dressing-gown. Eyes blazing with indignation she fumbled in her bag and fished out her identity card. The officer seemed to have no wish to see it. This made Gran even angrier. She flourished it.

There had been great trouble over her identity card when the Germans said everyone must have a new one, with a photograph. It seemed pointless in Gran's case. She never stirred out, and how was she to get a photograph? In the end, as Dad knew the photographer, he'd come to the house without extra charge. Once the fuss was over, Gran was quite proud of the document. Now, having at last got the chance to display it to a German, she was vexed that he showed so little interest.

Mum tried to smooth things over.

'My mother – you can see – is not well! She should not be upset!' Mum was shouting, most unlike her, thinking the officer would understand English better if it was loud. 'She's rather old now – '

'I am not old,' interrupted Gran. 'I am elderly.'

The officer took the card, glanced at her age, bowed and handed it back.

'Not a *bad* likeness,' said Gran chattily. 'Doesn't flatter me.' She scowled at the sergeant-major. 'What's *he* writing? Marches in without knocking! Outrageous! What can you expect from a Hun?'

'*Mother!*' pleaded Mrs Le Grand. 'You'll get us all into the most awful trouble.' She turned to Paul. 'Tell them Gran's under the doctor.'

Paul stood petrified. Even the simplest German words went completely out of his head – which was perhaps as well, for the officer responded quickly to sign-language as soon as Paul clapped a hand over where he supposed his own heart to be, and pointed to Gran.

'*Ja, Ja,*' said the officer sympathetically, and dictated something to the sergeant-major who noted it sulkily on his clipboard. Then with a bow he withdrew and they left the house without even looking at the attics above.

They heard no more about billeting. But they heard – and saw – a great deal more of the sergeant-major. Several other houses in the terrace were commandeered for soldiers, who used to parade in the roadway with much shouting and stamping. The sergeant-major became known locally as Horrible Hermann, from his resemblance to the equally massive and unlovable Marshal Goering, Hitler's righthand man.

* * *

The occupation, like the autumn weather, got grimmer. Not only food was short. Stocks of everything dwindled.

Lucy said how difficult it was at the shop. Cut off from England, the manager had to find suppliers of medicines and toilet articles in France or even Germany. In the depleted book department the German police had seized scores of Penguin paperbacks. 'Reckoned they were subversive,' she said scornfully. 'Critical of their blooming Reich!'

The censorship could be comic. At the school end-of-term concert a teacher was going to sing *Kiss me goodnight, Sergeant-Major*. The German authorities banned this popular song as it showed 'lack of respect for military rank'. After that, whenever Paul and George met Hermann strutting along the terrace, they whistled the tune in secret mockery.

Yet the occupation was no joke. That autumn two British officers were caught in Guernsey. The Germans announced that unless all those who had helped them could be traced, twenty leading islanders would be shot. In the end it did not come to that, but Major Sherwill and a number of others were sent away for a time to prison in France.

One day Miss Grimbly asked Paul to wait after the History lesson. Christmas was drawing near and she was sure that he could use a little extra pocket-money. He agreed eagerly. With prices rocketing and shops half-empty, buying presents was going to be a problem.

'You look a good strong boy for your age,' said Miss Grimbly. On Sundays, she explained, she played the organ in church. She liked to practise during the week. But with all the appeals to economise on electricity she felt she ought to find someone to blow the organ for her by hand. As there was no afternoon school on Thursdays, she wondered if. . . .

Miss Grimbly was a funny old thing, but he liked her and was glad to oblige. He could do with the money. His parents thoroughly approved.

He reached the church in good time. Miss Grimbly's ancient bicycle was in the porch. He went inside, instinctively on tiptoe as the religious atmosphere enveloped him.

Faint music came to him as he advanced down the aisle – which was slightly odd. Was she after all treating herself to a little electric power? Odder still, it was not organ music. It was a piano and a fiddle, more than one fiddle. . . .

Mystified, he crept up the wooden stairs to the organ-loft. To his relief it was Miss Grimbly sitting there, eyes closed, her usually stern features relaxed in blissful contentment. The music was coming from a portable wireless set in an open cupboard at her feet.

The stairs creaked under him. She was instantly alert. 'Ah, Paul!' She raised a warning finger. He froze. The music reached a climax, then hauntingly died away. A man's voice spoke smoothly, but she bent forward and switched it off. She closed the cupboard. 'So, you've discovered my little secret, Paul.'

'That was the BBC,' he whispered. He had never imagined Miss Grimbly breaking the law.

'I must have my music. And the news. But I have a

friend staying with me until her flat is ready. She's of a nervous disposition – we have a German post on the cliffs quite near my cottage, so I do not like to upset her.'

'I won't breathe a word,' he promised.

'Good boy. Now to work. Let me show you.'

He had never seen an organ at close quarters. He stared at the keyboard, the pedals, the projecting stops, the Great manual and the Swell manual, with strange names on each, Bourdon, Open Diapason, Viol da Gamba, and a lot more. He peeped into the mirror, tilted so that the organist could look down the length of the church.

She showed him the bellows handle on the left side. It wasn't heavy to work, she said, but you couldn't pause. 'You must pump for just a little while before I can start to play.'

'How long, Miss Grimbly?'

'See this weight dangling? It moves up and down to show there's enough air for the pipes. Go by that. And you mustn't stop until the music has finished.'

He gripped the polished wooden handle and set to work, watching the suspended weight. It was simple, though it might get tiring after a time. It was like pumping water – but very soon he found himself pumping music, glorious music that flowed out in waves through the church. 'Well,' she said with a chuckle, in answer to his comment, 'it *was* Handel's *Water Music*, after all.'

To give him a breather she opened the cupboard again and switched on the radio. General Wavell was stemming the Italian advance in the Western Desert. More raids on English cities, many Nazi bombers shot down . . . 'Let's get back to music,' she said.

She had to play for a wedding on Saturday. There weren't many weddings now. Most young men had left before the Germans arrived. 'I must brush up my Mendelssohn,' she said. He bent to his task again and she played the Wedding March from *Midsummer Night's Dream*. When the last notes had died away she whispered, 'I think we have an audience.'

She pointed to her mirror. In the long shadowy vista of empty pews he saw a solitary figure. Even in the November gloom there was no mistaking the uniform.

How long had the man been there? Could he have heard the radio voice? Suddenly the church seemed even colder.

Miss Grimbly was unruffled. She ran over one or two more pieces, a hymn, and something she called a 'voluntary', by Beethoven. To play when people were going out. Then she said, 'Thank you, Paul, that will do for this week.' She snicked open her purse, paid him, pulled on her gloves, and led the way down from the loft.

The soldier had waited. It was Oberleutnant Fischer. 'Thank you for the music. So beautifully played.'

Miss Grimbly bowed her head in formal acknowledgement. 'I am glad you enjoyed it,' she said, not very warmly. Though she had seen him in the school he had no cause to visit her own lessons.

'The Wedding March! I have not heard it for years.'

'Naturally,' she said crisply. 'Your Führer would not let you. Mendelssohn was a Jew.'

'Nevertheless – ' Fischer's voice was wistful. 'The music is so fine.'

She became more cordial. 'I shall continue to play it –

until your people clap me in jail.'

He gave an embarrassed laugh. 'No one would wish to do that. Certainly you have nothing to fear from me.'

Was it fancy, Paul wondered, or were his words loaded with special meaning? Had he heard the BBC voice? Was he reassuring them that he would not report it?

He walked with them down the path, discussing composers with Miss Grimbly. Then he saluted and strode away.

'That young man knows all about it,' she said approvingly. She meant, Paul realised, all about music.

She mounted her venerable machine and set off, wobbling but determined, to climb the hill to her cottage.

9

By Christmas the wartime shortages were really beginning to bite.

It was hard to explain to the smaller children. Tessa's brothers made her write long letters for them to Santa Claus. She did so with a heavy heart. Most of their requests were quite impossible to fulfil.

To prepare them for disappointment she added: *Do not come if it is dangerous. We should hate you to be shot down by mistake. We shall quite understand if you cannot make it.* The boys agreed grudgingly and scrawled their names over a line of crosses. Frank said that even a German gunner should be able to tell a reindeer sledge from a Blenheim bomber.

It was awkward having a father who was a respected public official and a stickler for the regulations. Father would have no dealings in the black market. Whereas Paul's father received all sorts of presents from satisfied customers – a chicken here, a bottle of whisky there – Mr Gray would accept nothing except from old friends or family. 'I daren't, in my position,' he explained, 'or people will think I bend the rules in return for favours.'

The Grays' Christmas would have been more of a famine than a festivity – but for Uncle Percy. He was Mrs

Gray's favourite brother, and Tessa's favourite uncle. He had a humorous weather-beaten face and wild hair sticking up in a cockatoo tuft, a gangling figure, always shabby, with mysteriously bulging pockets and mud-smeared boots.

He was not Mr Gray's favourite brother-in-law. Tessa's father called him 'feckless' while her mother defended him as 'sometimes weak'. Privately Tessa thought that Uncle Percy was as tough as his filthy old boots.

He was the black sheep of the family. It did not matter that he was a fisherman when every one else was in business or a safe job with a pension. Uncle Percy hadn't even a share in a boat. He was a 'casual', turning his hand to all sorts of things ashore when he wasn't at sea. That meant very often now, with all the restrictions the Germans had brought in. But he always found something, driving a lorry or helping out on a farm. Sometimes he would drink too much and sing loudly as he trudged along the waterfront. An embarrassing brother-in-law for a stiff-collared black-coated official in Public Health. . . .

However, he saved their Christmas. It was he who magically produced raisins when Mother was at her wits' end over the pudding, he who slipped into her kitchen with a fine joint of pork that had never seen a ration-book.

'Percy!' she cried gratefully. 'Though how on earth I'll explain it to Albert – '

'Say I found it in the net, fishing.' Uncle Percy's eyes danced in his poker face. 'Sorry it wasn't a turkey. The turkey shoals were swimming further out, over towards

66

Ushant.'

'You are a rogue, Percy!' She kissed him.

Both families could count one blessing that Christmas: they were all together, unlike so many others. Mr and Mrs Hopkins hadn't heard a word of Bill or his sisters since the evacuation. They might all have been killed in the air raids. It was agonising, with no letters and the mainland telephone cables cut. There was talk of the Red Cross trying to arrange for short messages through a neutral country, but nothing had been fixed yet.

For Paul the highlight of that Christmas was his new bicycle. Not really 'new', but new to him, polished up and fitted with good brakes and tyres. His old machine was absurdly small, for he'd shot up lately, but he'd given up hope of getting another. Dad had done a deal with a customer and there on Christmas morning was the wonderful glistening surprise.

His heart leapt. Just wait till spring! And the long summer days, the white lanes ribboning away under the green trees, framing distant segments of blue sea!

Long before those happy days arrived the blow fell: a grim official form, *'by order of the Commandant of the German Forces.'* His bicycle – *his* precious bicycle – was requisitioned. He must hand it in not later than Saturday, or incur alarming penalties.

He rode it to school that day. He could not bear to be parted from it. Slippery was unusually sympathetic. 'You're never going to let the Nazis have a super bike like this?'

'What else can I do?'

Slippery's eyes narrowed. 'What this bike wants is a

thorough overhaul.'

'Overhaul?' Paul echoed indignantly. 'Dad had it all done up for me! Good as new!'

'I know just the man for this job. After school.'

Lessons over, he led the way into a maze of winding alleys, stopping at a junk-shop stacked with time-worn objects of every sort. One notice said, *ANTIQUES*, another *REPAIRS OF ALL KINDS UNDERTAKEN*. A bent little figure emerged from the muddle. He greeted Slippery with a wary friendliness, the best attitude to Slippery till you knew what he was after.

'Got any tyres, Mr Lambert? Or brake-blocks?'

'In these days? Must be joking, young Stevie!'

'It's for my friend.' Slippery told the sad story.

'A-ah, that's different. Have to see, won't I?'

Mr Lambert rummaged in the murky recesses of his establishment. He came back with two unspeakably ancient tyres.

'You got to hand in your bike, lad, but no need to waste good tyres on the Germans.'

'No,' said Paul dejectedly. Mr Lambert might give him a bit for them, but what use was mere money?

'Leave it here till Thursday. I'll see what I can do. A thorough overhaul, eh?' He gave a cracked chuckle. 'You won't know your bike when you see it again.'

He was right. When Paul collected it two days later he could have wept. His beloved bicycle looked like a museum exhibit. The tyres were worn smooth, the handlebars chipped and taken, like the rusty chain, from another machine. The brakes did not work. The saddle had been replaced with a damaged one which threatened permanent anatomical injury.

'I've kept all your own bits and pieces,' said Mr Lambert, 'just in case they don't want your bike after all. If so, bring it back.'

As Paul wheeled the ruin away he said to Slippery, 'Mr Lambert's a crafty one.'

'I'll say! Been making antique furniture for years.'

Paul decided to hand in the machine at once. He did not want to be associated with it in its altered guise. He pushed it shamefacedly through the back streets. It would have been risky to ride it.

A few days later came a second official letter. His bicycle was not after all required. He could collect it.

He thanked Slippery almost with tears in his eyes. 'That's O.K.,' said Slippery. 'You'd do the same for me.'

Scoring off the Germans had become a popular sport. The occupation was now more and more resented.

There was bitter feeling over Major Sherwill. After harsh solitary confinement in France he had been allowed to come home, but not to take up his public position again. He bore his punishment philosophically. He dug his garden and, no longer having any salary on which to keep his family, was not too proud to sell his vegetables. He might be seen, with a cheerful grin, pushing his laden wheelbarrow along the street.

But worse things were in store.

One day the German lesson was interrupted by the headmaster. He murmured something to Miss Goldsmith. The sharp-eared front row caught the words 'police' and 'identity card'.

'You see?' said Slippery during the break. 'Always said there was something fishy about her.'

'You said she was a Nazi spy,' Tessa retorted. 'The police wouldn't be bothering her if she was.'

Goldilocks wore an anxious look that day, but soon recovered her vivacity. Her lessons continued to be popular, rivalled only by Miss Grimbly's unconventional version of history.

Then one Saturday morning, a few weeks later, George put up his hand and inquired about the homework for Monday. Goldilocks had scarcely smiled throughout the lesson. Her eyes had an odd look, and Tessa realised afterwards that she must have been crying.

'Homework?' she said. 'Of course . . . homework.' Her voice trembled. 'Revise. I shall not be taking you on Monday. I shall not be teaching you any more.'

The bell in the corridor went *drrring*. Before the stunned class could fire a question she was gone. No one was supposed to run in the corridor. Miss Goldsmith did.

10

'Mark my words,' said Slippery in the playground afterwards. 'She's in trouble with the cops.' That was something he had always managed most skilfully to avoid.

'Not Goldilocks!' said George. 'Why should she be?'

'Passing under a false name.' Slippery's tone was triumphant. The others exclaimed in disbelief. 'I just happened to see her identity card the other day.'

'You "just happened"?' said Tessa.

'During break. She'd left her bag on her desk. I knocked it off accidentally – *honest*! So I picked it up – she wouldn't want her stuff spilt all over the floor – '

'She wouldn't want you going through it, either.'

'I never! I was only pushing her identity card back in. I thought I'd just see how old she was.'

'And how old *is* she?' they all cried, curiosity overcoming their good manners.

Slippery grinned. 'Twenty-two. Born Salzburg, Austria, 1919. And her name's Rosa.'

'Lovely,' said one of the girls.

'But her surname's not "Goldsmith". It's "Goldschmidt".'

'That's not a false name,' said Paul, 'it's just their

spelling. Foreigners often change their names when they settle in Britain.'

'And she never pretended to be British,' said Tessa.

Slippery was eager to hold his audience. 'There was a word stamped across her card in big red letters. *JUDAS*. If that doesn't mean "traitor" – '

An idea occurred to Tessa. 'Sure the word was Judas? Not *J-U-D-E-N*?'

'What's that mean?' George asked. 'Is it German?'

It was not a word Goldilocks had taught them. But Tessa had grown keen on the subject and picked up other words as she leafed through the dictionary. 'I think it means "Jewish".'

They looked at each other with anxiety. This could be serious. They knew that the Nazis persecuted Jews. Even here in Guernsey some horrific tales of cruelty had filtered through.

Suddenly one or two little things began to make sense. Strange looks, odd remarks, that had passed between Goldilocks and Oberleutnant Fischer. He had detected her Jewishness? And she had known that he knew? And they had been soft enough to imagine that he was getting sweet on her! Now the explanation might be more sinister.

Back home, Tessa tackled her father. He looked uncomfortable. 'I believe some weeks ago the Germans asked for a list of Jews on the island. Our police had to comply. I think there were only three or four. Their cards had to be specially stamped.'

'Will anything happen to them?'

'They may have to leave Guernsey.'

'Where will they go? Not one of those awful camps?'

'I – I don't know. We mustn't *ask* these questions.' She saw he was quite agitated. 'It does no good,' he said. 'It could get us into the most appalling trouble. It's not our business.'

'Isn't it?' she said disbelievingly.

'*We're* not Jews,' said her mother, 'we're Christians.'

'Are we?' said Tessa.

Monday came. Of course, there was no Miss Goldsmith. Her lesson was taken by the French mistress, who clearly did not know much German and was only keeping one step ahead of the class.

Oberleutnant Fischer chose that very day for a visit. He looked surprised and disappointed. His expression grew glummer and glummer. It might have been due to the absence of Goldilocks or to the inept performance of her substitute. After a dreary twenty minutes the door opened again.

Mr Dexter hurried in, followed by one of the island policemen. They looked as amazed to see Fischer as he was to see them. Mr Dexter conferred with him in low tones. The German looked horrified. The constable was searching Miss Goldsmith's desk.

'No sign of a note here, sir. Only the usual stuff.'

They went out. Fischer followed and did not come back. The lesson limped on. Nobody learnt anything. Yet in another sense it was a lesson that nobody ever forgot.

By evening rumours were flying round the town. The pretty young Austrian teacher had vanished from her lodgings. Some said she had been a British agent, others that she had been carrying on a secret love-affair. No one knew much about her. Her fellow-teachers were tight-lipped.

Paul's mother cleared up one point for her troubled son. She knew a woman who worked as cleaner for Miss Goldsmith's landlady. Of course nobody had known the girl for long – she'd arrived in Guernsey only a few days before the evacuation – but everyone agreed, she was 'as nice a young lady as you could wish to meet'.

'*We* know that, Mum. But why did she suddenly come here? It's so mysterious.'

No mystery, said his mother. She'd escaped when Hitler invaded Austria. So very likely she *was* Jewish. She'd become a governess to a rich family in London. They'd brought her on holiday to Alderney. When the war in France began to hot up, they'd decided to go to Canada. But, being Austrian, Miss Goldsmith was reckoned as an "enemy alien", and couldn't get a permit to enter Canada. She had to stay behind. The Guernsey teaching job had seemed a wonderful bit of luck.

'But what's happened to her, Mum?'

'That I can't say. Seems to be a mystery *there*.'

Tessa's father knew little more. 'It seems there were four of them,' he said that evening. 'They were to report this morning and be taken across to St Malo. One never turned up. That must have been your teacher.'

The vital question remained unanswered. But not for long.

The next day the school was buzzing. Miss Goldsmith had been last seen walking alone on Sunday afternoon. On Monday a search of her lodgings had revealed a letter.

No one knew what it had said, but every one could guess. It could only have been a suicide note. Knowing the fate of so many Jewish victims before her, Rosa Goldsmith had preferred to end her life in her own way.

Sure enough, that evening, a soldier patrolling a cliff path came upon a neatly folded jacket that was quickly identified as hers. It was several days before a shoe was sighted at low tide in the rocky cove far beneath, but because of the barbed wire and buried mines the police did not try to recover it.

The tragic story was all over the island. There was nothing, however, in Gran's paper. The censor saw to that.

11

There was so much sadness in those months that the death of one young woman, an unknown foreigner, was soon forgotten.

At school, though, it was not so. Every German lesson was a reminder. A more competent replacement was found, but that period was never again the highlight of the school day. Fischer merely dropped in once for a few minutes.

Paul met him, however, soon after the suicide, when he came to listen to Miss Grimbly's organ-playing. He was a welcome visitor now. There was no longer the difficulty of a hidden radio. Now and for the next eighteen months the islanders were permitted to have their wireless sets again. In any case Miss Grimbly no longer had her nervous friend staying in her cottage. She was free also to get on with some long-postponed redecoration, and gave Paul a message asking his father to call upon her.

That was the afternoon Fischer appeared at her rehearsal. He waited as usual to thank her. She had ended with a short piece that was very plaintive and haunting. He was reminded of Beethoven, he said.

She nodded. 'There's a deliberate echo of his Sonata in C Minor. But the music's from the *Enigma Variations* –

Elgar. An Englishman – but one who loved Germany. The 1914 war almost broke his heart. We often play this piece at funerals, when we are thinking of a special friend.' She gave him a very straight look.

His fair skin flushed darkly. 'War is terrible.'

'I am glad you realise that.'

Paul's father went up to see her and was well pleased with the work she gave him. The only problem was materials.

'It's not just her new bookshelves,' he said. 'She wants alterations, a real building job. Cement's the problem.'

Sand and gravel were easy. He knew a beach that was still open and unmined. He could load a truck when nobody was about. Cement was another matter.

Tessa's Uncle Percy came to the rescue. Between fishing trips he was now driving lorries for the Germans who were constantly building concrete pillboxes and gun emplacements. 'I can get you cement any time,' he said. 'Amazing what falls off those German lorries!'

'And I bet the bags never burst,' said Mr Le Grand.

'Fifty marks a load, delivered? On a dark night. I work late, you see. Very industrious, I am.'

It was not the way Paul's father would have chosen to do business, but how else could one keep going nowadays?

That summer term the war took a new direction. Without warning, Hitler attacked Russia. It was another blitzkrieg on a gigantic scale, a tidal wave of tanks pouring over the frontier eastwards.

Tessa sat with her parents on that Sunday evening, waiting for Winston Churchill's broadcast to the nation.

What would he say? He had always been anti-Communist as well as anti-Nazi. How would he feel now that he found himself with the dictator Stalin as an ally?

When the well-known voice came over the air they were not left in doubt for a moment. 'We must speak out now at once, without a day's delay. . . . We are resolved to destroy Hitler and every vestige of the Nazi regime. . . . Any man or state who fights on against Nazidom will have our aid. . . . We shall give whatever help we can to Russia and the Russian people.'

Tessa thrilled to the Prime Minister's rolling eloquence. But her father was a little discouraging. He distrusted the Russians. He thought them badly organized and technically backward, no good as allies. The Germans would walk over them. Tessa's spirits drooped again.

For some weeks it seemed that Mr Gray was right. Even the BBC said that the Red Army was falling back and had lost vast tracts of territory. Yet somehow the Russian collapse never came. New hope rose in the West. The Nazis *could* be beaten. One day Europe *would* be free.

Even in Guernsey people heard of the new 'V for Victory' slogan and daubed the letter everywhere, defying the German ban.

One morning during break the fat sergeant-major rode into the playground, propped his bicycle against the railings, and stormed in demanding to see the headmaster. A whisper went round: last night some one had chalked a V on an army billet. Boys had been seen running away.

It was long after break when Hermann departed.

Through the open classroom window Paul heard Mr Dexter's farewell promise, 'If I catch any boy doing such a thing I will deal with him most severely.'

Paul stole a glance through the window. He saw Hermann strutting away, saw him grasp his handlebars and throw a massive leg over the saddle – and saw him stop after a yard or two, dismount, feel his back tyre, and then glare back across the empty playground. For a moment it looked as though the man would come storming back into the school. Instead, he unclipped his pump and bent over the wheel.

Gleefully Paul now saw something else – a clear white V in chalk, transferred from the saddle to the expansive seat of Hermann's breeches. He had no idea who had played the trick. He could only pray that Hermann would never discover. When the sergeant-major went strutting among his men again, they would enjoy the joke as much as any one. The credit (Paul learnt afterwards) was George Gasson's.

Even Miss Grimbly introduced the forbidden sign into her organ-playing. One afternoon she broke into the opening bars of Beethoven's Fifth Symphony. Da-da-da-*dah*! Da-da-da-*DAH*!

Paul recognised those notes as the BBC call-sign to occupied Europe. The Roman numeral five was V. The Morse code matching the notes, dot-dot-dot-dash, spelt the same letter V.

Fischer, listening at the back of the church, knew too. He said nothing afterwards. What *could* he say? It was Beethoven's music and Beethoven was a German.

'It was rather naughty of me,' Miss Grimbly confessed

later. 'I suspect that poor Mr Fischer is no more a Nazi than I am. But he is a soldier, and he has to obey orders.'

Autumn came. Paul and Tessa moved up into a new form. Early in the term they were brought face to face with the war again. A German convoy had anchored in the roadstead in front of the town; tugs, barges and merchant vessels. Paul was chatting in Gran's room one evening, when the RAF struck. Out of a cloudless sky a dozen fighters swooped screaming over the harbour, bombs bursting, machine–guns stuttering.

'Lie flat!' Paul yelled. He was thinking of the window – the murderous glass splinters. He dropped beside Gran's bed, pulled a pillow over her face. No time to do anything else. No time to be really frightened. The raid was over in a minute.

Gran threw aside the pillow. 'What you want to do a thing like that for?' she demanded indignantly. 'Finish me off?' He explained. 'Oh, you're a good boy,' she conceded gratefully. She sat up and peered eagerly through the unbroken window.

Flames and dense smoke billowed up from the anchored convoy. Two barges and a tug were sinking. Germans dashed frenziedly along the waterfront.

That brief raid put new heart into every one. Britain was beginning to hit back. The Russians were still holding out.

'If only the Yanks would come in!' said Dad, wistfully. President Roosevelt was giving Churchill all the help he dared, but most Americans wanted to keep out of the war.

* * *

In October new ration books were issued. 'Though what use they are, *I* don't know,' said Mum despondently. Supplies of tea and cocoa had almost given out. Some weeks there was no meat. Potatoes might not last beyond Christmas. The sweet ration had ceased entirely; the milk allocation was reduced.

More troops poured into the island. Nearly twenty thousand now, Dad heard. And forced labourers as well, French, Polish, Russian, all sorts, building new fortifications. No more talk of invading England. Hitler was too tied up in Russia. He was concerned only to protect his rear from the British.

So more and more Guernsey people were turned out of their homes to provide billets. The Grays and Le Grands were lucky: George Gasson's family had to crowd in with relatives.

Then in December, without warning, Japan attacked the American Pacific fleet at Pearl Harbor and the British naval bases in the Far East. To support his Japanese friends Hitler declared war on the United States.

The first news was numbing. Disaster after disaster. In the Le Grand household only Dad was cheerful. 'I'm sorry for the Yanks,' he said, 'but for us it's wonderful.'

'I don't see – ' Lucy began.

'*You're* only thinking, we've got another enemy. Look at it this way: we've got another ally. With the Yanks on our side we can't lose. In the long run.'

'In the long run!' Gran sniffed. 'How far you expect *me* to run?'

'You'll be all right. We all shall. Mark my words.'

So they entered another dreary winter of war. 'Never

mind,' said Dad, 'we're better off than the Jerries in Russia. Freezing to death in thousands *they* are.'

As the BBC kept repeating, the Red Army now had 'General Winter' fighting for them. The Germans had been confident of a swift summer victory. They hadn't the clothing needed for sub-Arctic temperatures. They were suffering phenomenal casualties.

The result was seen even in Guernsey. Units were constantly moving out and being replaced. The tough-looking young men who had swaggered about St Peter Port in the early days were being changed for elderly reservists and immature youths.

One Thursday Tessa had to fetch some eggs that Uncle Percy said would be waiting for collection at a farm outside the town. She must not go until it was dark. It was not far, and she was not nervous, but to reassure her mother she arranged that Paul would go with her. She would meet him at the church after Miss Grimbly's practice.

She arrived in good time. The music was still rolling gloriously round the twilit building. She was not surprised to see Fischer sitting there. She knew of his visits. She slipped into a seat behind him, knelt, covered her eyes with her hands, and murmured a prayer. At least, she thought wryly, her gloves were holey.

That was one of the things about the war that hit girls more than boys. Clothes. Not just threadbare gloves. Everything. The impossibility of getting anything *new*. It was bad enough for growing boys like Paul, who now seemed all bony wrists and ankles. If they were not bursting out of their own old clothes they were submerged in voluminous garments handed down by their elders.

Worse for girls, though. It wasn't just the fit, it was the lack of anything pretty and exciting. She thought wistfully of the pre-war days. She'd been small then, but her mother used to say she had 'dress sense'. She'd loved the Saturday afternoon shopping, window-gazing, choosing materials and paper patterns. Then the cosy evenings by the fire, the whirring of Mother's machine after the careful cutting and pinning, then the first thrill of trying on something new.

The music died away. Fischer stood up, turned and recognised her in the gloom. 'Ah, Tessa – Gray, yes? The girl who is good at German!'

'I don't know about that, sir.' She had stuck at her work, but the lessons were no longer fun. *He* knew that. 'When are you coming to test us again, sir?'

'Never, I fear,' he said quietly.

'*Never?*' She was surprised at the woe in her voice.

'I am posted to the Eastern Front.'

She caught her breath. 'Russia?' A word of doom.

'I should not tell you, it is what we call a "troop movement", top secret! But perhaps we shall meet again in happier times. So – what do we say in German?'

His last, childishly easy question. '*Auf wiedersehen,*' she faltered. 'Full marks,' he said, and patted her shoulder, as Miss Grimbly and Paul came down the aisle.

12

'These are the times that try men's souls,' Miss Grimbly declaimed sternly to the History class.

She was telling them about the American War of Independence, quoting what Tom Paine had written in the dark hours when it looked as though George Washington might be beaten by the redcoats. Now that America was in the war as an ally, British children should know her history too.

'*I* was taught nothing as a child,' she said scornfully, 'except that Washington, when a boy, chopped down a tree and then owned up.' In a namby-pamby voice she parodied the immortal line, 'Father, I cannot tell a lie.' Becoming Miss Grimbly again she said, 'He was lucky not to be growing up in Guernsey in 1942.'

They all knew what she meant. Who in the island could survive if they always told the exact truth? In June the Germans had finally confiscated all radios. Yet, mysteriously, many people knew what the BBC had said the night before. They knew the latest song hits in Britain. They knew the voice of Vera Lynn, 'the Forces' sweetheart', with her crooning refrain:

> *There'll be blue birds over*
> *The white cliffs of Dover*

Tomorrow – just you wait and see!

Some had never handed in their radios or had kept back a portable. Friendly workshops and garages would recharge batteries, no questions asked. Other people searched their lumber for long-discarded crystal-sets and headphones. Or recalled their schoolday skills, when many a boy had made his own receiver from cigar-box wood, a crystal from the science lab, and a few oddments.

The illicit radios were hidden under floorboards and in disused kitchen-ranges, in upholstered armchairs and sofas, even in rabbit-hutches. The undertaker kept his in a coffin.

Shortage of news was one thing. Other shortages were harder to remedy.

Paul and Tessa and their friends spent much time gathering anything that would help to eke out the food ration. Now they picked not only blackberries but basketfuls of their leaves which, dried and chopped, made a pathetic substitute for tea. Parsnips could be roasted and grated instead of coffee-beans. If you had no parsnips you had to look for oak trees in the fields and lanes, and gather acorns instead. Sometimes Frank and Harold joined in these expeditions, but their shorter legs soon tired, and they grew bored.

As a little boy Paul had enjoyed searching for shellfish at low tide. Now there were few beaches open. You were lucky if you could find enough limpets to make into a sort of brawn, or fill a basket with carrageen moss off the rocks. This seaweed was edible and could be turned into a jelly.

Another regular habit was to hang about at an awkward street-corner where the German supply trucks passed and the drivers often had to pull up sharply. Sometimes things really fell off by accident, a loaf of bread, a few potatoes bouncing out of their big wicker baskets and rolling down the gutter, or a glistening lump of coal. More frequently, if the lorry-driver was a Guernsey man or there was even a kindly German, the falling objects were given a little help, and the watchful boys and girls were quick to pounce.

Paul's ancient long-forgotten pram came back into service. He went into partnership with Tessa and they would push it to the Old Harbour at low tide, when lumps of coal could be picked out of the mud. The pram was useful too for collecting fallen branches and furze from the country lanes.

Gran hated to think of Paul out in all weathers, scrounging for fuel and food to eke out supplies. 'I'll never forgive those Germans,' she said vehemently. 'They've taken your childhood! The best years of your life. They can't ever be given back to you.'

'That's all right, Gran,' he said uncomfortably. 'We don't have such a bad time. Honest.'

He did not tell her the worst things. Like being booted off the pavement by Hermann and once feeling the lash of his whip. A crowd of them had been loitering round a gateway where the German trucks pulled up to unload. There was quite often something to be picked up sooner or later if you were smart enough. But the sergeant-major noticed that, and had taken to appearing suddenly with an ugly whip. You had to be careful. The soldiers, too, became more careful. It was surprising now how little fell into the roadway.

Slippery seldom joined the gang. 'You gotta think big,' he told his schoolfellows scornfully. Tessa reckoned that one of Slippery's big thoughts was a forged ration book. She had always disapproved of Slippery, but she found it harder now to adopt a high moral line.

There was her own Uncle Percy. She never knew when she would find him in the kitchen, except that it wouldn't be when her father was at home.

Not only was Uncle Percy always dropping in, he was usually dropping *something* in. Once he entered empty-handed, but his huge boots proved to be full of flour. He sat there in his stockinged feet, tipping it into a clean pillow-case Tessa held open. He'd been driving German supplies from the quay. 'A bag somehow got spilt,' he said with a wink. 'Shame to waste it.'

It was the ingenuity of fooling the enemy that appealed to him. When he went out fishing there were other tricks to play.

The Germans thought they had the fishermen under strict control. They could not put to sea without taking their special identity cards and permits to the watch-house on the quay. Each boat had to carry an armed soldier to see that they didn't try to escape and head for England. It gave Uncle Percy a mischievous pleasure to stay out longer in rough weather until their escort was helplessly sick.

He had a poor opinion of the Germans when it came to their understanding of the sea. 'Had to teach 'em about *tides*,' he said. 'They wanted to fix times for everything, when we could do this and when we could do that. As if we were buses! Had to teach 'em that tides come different times every day.'

When the boats came in again, they had to check in at the watch-house and declare their catch. They had to hand over a fixed proportion to the Germans. Uncle Percy was very cunning when it came to reporting the weight of the fish caught.

Paul loved Tessa's stories of her wicked uncle. She swore him to secrecy. She wouldn't have told any other boy, barring George Gasson. Certainly not Slippery.

She remembered Miss Grimbly's story of George Washington. *He* wouldn't have lasted long under the Nazis. In today's world the expert liar was the man you were forced to admire. Lying and stealing were your only weapons against Nazis.

Paul's grandmother would snort over her newspaper. 'Can't think what's come over the farmers. Can't they look after their animals nowadays?' She laid her brown old finger on the 'Lost' column. 'Such a list gone astray!'

'P'raps they've been stolen, Gran.'

'Shouldn't wonder, with the meat ration what it is. But this used to be an honest island. Seems now it's a den of thieves.' She knitted her brows. 'Where's the sense in advertising, though? The thieves won't bring 'em back just because there's a notice in the paper.'

'Those ads,' said Lucy, 'are only for the Jerries.'

'What d'ye mean, girl?'

'They know what every farmer's got – or think they do. If you kill a pig you have to report it and hand over half the meat. So people keep quiet and sell on the black

88

market. Then put the ad in the paper to pretend the animal is missing.'

'Never heard of such a thing!'

Tessa had. A few days later she took Paul aside. Uncle Percy had this farmer friend.... There'd be a parcel waiting for her mother tonight, but Tessa must fetch it. Children were best for such errands. The Germans did not watch their comings and goings. It must be after dark, though, as late as possible before the curfew. 'Would you –' she began, hesitantly.

'Course I would!'

He enjoyed the idea of a secret mission, secret not only from the enemy but also from Mr Gray. He would not approve of breaking the regulations – or of his daughter walking through the dark lanes with Paul.

It was a soft evening, for spring came early in Guernsey. They set out in the sunset glow. It did not matter what Germans they met on the outward journey. Tessa's footsteps clacked on the hard road. 'These *awful* shoes!' she said with a groan.

Like many girls at school she now had to wear wooden soles. Everyone's feet were growing; no one could buy new shoes of leather. And Tessa's mother was a neat little woman, and already Tessa took a larger size.

'You'll be heard all over the island,' said Paul.

'I'll be all right coming back. I've brought a pair of Father's old football stockings. I'll pull 'em over on top.'

As they turned up the long track to the farm they met two boys from school. They were on bicycles, hurrying home before lighting-up time. They came bumping painfully over the sun-hardened ruts, *kerlump, kerlump*, their makeshift tyres mere rope and strips of hosepipe. They made more noise than Tessa.

At the kitchen-door Tessa murmured Uncle Percy's magic name. The farmer's wife invited them in, a gaunt, wispy-haired old woman, businesslike but kindly. She vanished into the larder and returned with a package wrapped in newspaper. Tessa counted out the money in the soft light of the oil lamp. The woman turned to Paul.

'And who might you be?' He told her. 'I know your dad,' she said, 'a nice man to deal with. Hang on, let's see what we can manage. How many of you are there?'

'Five,' he said.

She went back to the larder. 'I could let you have three chops. Otherwise it's all spoken for.'

Three chops! Mum would be thrilled. She'd get a tasty meal out of them for the whole family. He fumbled in his pocket. With his organ-blowing money he could cover the price. He thanked the farmer's wife and she rolled up the chops in newspaper.

There were hasty footsteps in the yard. A tap on the door, and a young woman rushed into the kitchen.

'Some Jerries stopped me in the road! But they only wanted to know if I'd seen a man they were looking for. One of those Polish workers, they said, dark and tall. As if I'd have told them if I *had* seen him!'

Guernsey people seldom saw much of the slave labourers, Polish and Russian prisoners mostly, with a few Frenchmen, Algerians and others. They were herded away in their camps, marched out at first dawn, toiling long hours on the fortifications. They were half-starved, living like animals, working till they dropped. Now and again one broke out, but in so small an island it was impossible to remain on the run for long. Escapers were tracked down, taken back, and flogged unmercifully.

'The Jerries have set up a road-block just outside the town,' said the woman. 'They're stopping everybody.'

Tessa and Paul looked at each other. 'I've not come all this way to have it taken off me by a bunch of Nazis,' she said.

'There's the cliff path,' he said, doubtfully. Most of it was still open, with one diversion to avoid a gun-site and one or two other places where it was wiser to slip through the hedge to avoid a sentry. He knew the way well by daylight. But in the dark. . .

She read his thoughts. 'There'll be a moon – if the clouds break.'

'Let's get going, then.' The path would take longer than the road. They must be home before curfew.

'Mind how you go,' said the farmer's wife anxiously. 'And if you're stopped, mind you don't say –'

'We won't,' he promised, but with forebodings.

She set them on their way. It was just possible to see the lighter-coloured path across the meadow. A shadowy cow rose and lurched away into the gloom.

The next field brought them to the coastal track. They could hear the waves crashing and hissing below.

'This is exciting,' she whispered.

'I'll say!'

Barbed wire ran along the seaward side, but at the worst places where the ground fell in a sheer precipice the Germans had left it unguarded, reckoning that even a British commando could not scale the cliff. After one sickening slither near such a point Tessa remembered her father's football stockings and pulled them over her shoes to avoid another slip.

Ahead, they knew, lay a sandy cove – a picnic spot in happier days. Now, as an obvious landing-place, it had a German pillbox permanently manned. They must steer wide of that, leaving the coastal path, and striking down through a steep wooded valley that ran inland in a V shape with a stream burbling down to the beach.

In a few weeks it would be misty with bluebells. Paul knew its interlacing little pathways from countless games of hide-and-seek in his childhood. He still kept a mental picture of their lay-out. So, dark though it was, he led the way confidently, zigzagging down, occasionally thrusting out a hand to Tessa.

Once for a few moments the clouds parted. The treetops overhead made a black wrought-iron tracery against the brilliance of the moonlight. Below, far to their right, the pillbox glimmered whitely between the slender tree-trunks.

They heard voices down there. Jackboots and rifle-butts crashed on the concrete. 'They're sending out a patrol,' he hissed in her ear.

They had frozen where they stood. Was it better to stay there, praying that the soldiers would not come their way? Or press on, and get out of the valley as fast as they could? They hadn't unlimited time. There was that blasted curfew. . . . And tonight the soldiers were making a proper search for someone, not just a routine patrol. They'd comb the woods.

'Best get on,' he said softly. They stole down to the

stream, shallow but icy cold round their ankles. He led the way up the slope beyond. It was dark again.

Then, horrors! – above them a German voice barked a challenge. Paul stopped. She almost bumped into him. They stood rigid.

Thank God, the voice was not addressing them – it was being answered by another. Tessa's German was good enough to understand what was said. Two patrols must have run into each other, the one from the pillbox, the other from the town. Just our luck, she thought bitterly. The wood must be alive with soldiers.

Bad enough just to be caught! But what if they fired first and asked questions afterwards? She felt Paul's face hot against her own. He was whispering urgently.

'We'll have to go up the steep way. Quiet as you can!'

She followed him. The thick wool, stretched over her shoes, gave a reassuring grip on the slope.

Voices pealed across the valley, calling and answering, maintaining contact. She felt like a fish, frantically plunging and twisting in the meshes of a net.

Sometimes Paul braced himself with one arm round a tree, the other groping back to help her. 'Nearly at the top,' he breathed into her ear.

Had they made it? There were men crashing about above them to the right, no one immediately ahead – unless some one was standing there, silent. Suddenly she had an uncanny feeling that there was. She tugged Paul's sleeve. 'Wait. Some one in front.'

He listened. 'How do you know?' He was impatient to get this over. Irritable with fear.

Again the moon sailed through a tatter of parting

93

cloud. She saw the figure standing on the path above, motionless, staring intently down at her.

It was not a soldier. It was – in those first few seconds of incredulous realisation – something even more terrifying. The face of the dead.

13

Impossible! It couldn't be Goldilocks. Goldilocks had taken her own life, months and months ago, to avoid the horrors of a prison-camp.

Yet the voice was hers, sounding almost as frightened as Tessa herself. Yet relieved.

'I thought you were a Nazi! It *is* Tessa Gray?'

It was only the moon that had given her face that deathly pallor. The voice was alive and warm. So was the hand that stretched out and was placed on Tessa's lips.

'Sh! This way.'

Stealthily but confidently Miss Goldsmith flitted between the silvery tree-trunks. She had taken in Paul's presence too, for she beckoned him.

The night was still noisy with unseen trampling soldiers. Paul, himself unnerved by this uncanny recognition, wondered where the teacher was leading them. The moon slid behind a cloud. They could barely see each other in the gloom. They must not lose Goldilocks, but they must not trip in their haste and make some fatal sound.

They were getting near the crest of the slope. Soon the wood would thin out, they'd be in the open, in deadly danger if the moon came out again. But for the moment dense evergreens enclosed them, the sky was a solid black roof, unrelieved by a single star.

There was the faintest click. Goldilocks was steering them through a little gate. It was harder and smoother under their feet. Flagstones. They felt, rather than saw, the mass of a building looming over them. 'I am sorry, it is so prickly,' said their guide. She steered them gently, first to the right, then to the left. Paul thought of the phrase, 'pulled through a hedge backwards'. Goldilocks was doing it frontwards, though in the kindest way.

They were pressed against a rough stone wall. A pencil-thin torch-beam sprang from her hand, picking out a door, shabby and long unpainted, like the door of a shed or coalhouse. There was a roof of whitewashed brick arched over their heads, but still the open night and the thorny shrubs on one side. Paul was reminded of a cottage he had once been to, built on a steep slope overlooking the sea, with the living-room projecting on pillars, with a sort of basement below for garden-tools and coal-store. This seemed a rather similar place.

Goldilocks opened the shabby door. He had nerved himself for a great creaking and squeaking, but of course – he should have known! – the door opened silently on its well-oiled hinges. The torch revealed a narrow room, made narrower by a flight of stone steps rising into the gloom. Goldilocks closed the door behind them. The fresh night air gave place to a dankness, a lingering memory of meals. A match rasped and flared, a stub of candle flamed from a saucer. 'Now we can talk safely,' said the teacher.

There was a camp-bed. She sat down on it and patted

the space beside her for Tessa. 'The chair is for the gentleman,' she said. Paul took it. 'I am not accustomed to visitors,' she said. There was a hint of the old fun in her voice, but it broke suddenly as she turned to Tessa and hugged her impulsively. 'I am sorry, my dear – it has been so *long* – '

'Have you been here,' Paul asked, 'ever since. . . .'

'Ever since I pretended to kill myself? Yes. I must hide here during the day. I take the air only when it is dark.' They gasped in sympathy. 'It is usually safe. But tonight, for some reason – '

'One of the slave-workers has run away,' he said. He was longing to ask questions. So was Tessa, perched on the bed, devouring the teacher's face with her own round eyes.

'So. Now you know my secret – as they say in stories.'

'We shan't tell any one,' said Paul.

'Where *are* we?' Tessa asked. But Paul broke in again, 'Better not tell us, Miss Goldsmith!' They both knew the grim thought in his mind, but the matter was decided for them. A new voice spoke from the gloom at the top of the steps.

'Rosa! Are you all right?' It was Miss Grimbly.

Miss Goldsmith explained. 'Then you'd better bring them up,' said the music mistress. They mounted the steps. In a soft glow of lamplight stood Miss Grimbly, in an ancient but rather splendid dressing-gown. 'Mind your heads,' she said. They ducked under a beam and found themselves in a cosy sitting room. A black spaniel stirred on the hearthrug and let out a low growl.

'Quiet, Rupert!' ordered Miss Grimbly. 'He barks

only at the Occupying Forces. It is handy. It gives me time. And nobody expects a lonely old lady to be quick at answering the door-bell.' She waved them to seats.

Looking round the book-lined walls Paul was bewildered. A door stood open to the hall with its coat-pegs and umbrella-stand. There ought to be another door, a very low one, near the piano – that was where they had come in. But there were only bookshelves.

Miss Grimbly noted his look and chuckled. 'Some of your father's excellent workmanship.' She walked across, thrust a hand down behind the books, and the bottom five rows of shelving swung out to reveal the stone steps they had just climbed. 'Perfect fit, perfect balance, smooth and silent. I hope you are proud of your father.'

'Oh, I *am*. But I never knew about this!'

'I should hope not. He would never gossip about a customer's private arrangements. I knew I could trust him. And Miss Goldsmith was in terrible trouble. It was literally a matter of life and death.'

'I had truly decided to kill myself,' said the young Austrian earnestly. 'I wrote a letter – I meant it – '

'Yes, yes,' said Miss Grimbly hastily. 'But we must not burden the children with such dreadful things. Fortunately you talked to me.'

Afterwards Paul and Tessa were able to reconstruct the story themselves from what they learned that night. Goldilocks had really planned to throw herself over the cliff. Miss Grimbly had talked her out of it. They had faked the suicide. Paul's father had been brought into it to create a hiding-place.

He had made it out of the old fuel-store under the

cottage. The outside door, once needed for coal deliveries, had long been disused. A dense shrubbery masked its very existence. Similarly the stone steps leading up inside into the house had never been used since the days of strong servant girls who could carry up the heavy scuttles. Miss Grimbly kept a coal-bunker and a stack of logs beside the kitchen door. So why not wall off the unnecessary opening behind some extra bookcases – but leave it available for emergencies?

Tessa and Paul were fascinated. The miraculous return from the dead of Goldilocks was overwhelming enough, but that Miss Grimbly, and then Paul's father, had played the vital parts in her survival –

'There *are* no coincidences in Guernsey,' Miss Grimbly declared. 'The place is too small. We all know each other, anyhow.'

In their excitement they had lost their sense of time. When the clock chimed the half-hour Tessa cried in alarm: 'The curfew! We'll never get home – '

They all knew at once that she was right. Even without having to dodge road-blocks and patrols, they could never cover the distance in thirty minutes.

'You must stay here,' said Miss Grimbly.

'Oh, we *can't*. My mother will be frantic.'

'I will telephone, my dear.'

'We're not *on* the 'phone!'

'Paul's father is, for his business. If I ring at once he will just have time to warn your parents too.'

She marched out into the hall. Her precise tones came clearly back to them. 'Mrs Le Grand? Good-evening. This is Miss Grimbly. I have your boy here. No, no, he is quite all right. But it is late, and I understand the Germans are stopping people on the roads. He can't get home by curfew, so I think it best to keep him here for the night. . . . No, no trouble at all. I am glad you agree.'

Only a bold parent would not agree, thought Tessa, when Miss Grimbly was organizing things.

'One other thing, Mrs Le Grand. Could your husband step round to Tessa Gray's house, and say she too is here? Yes, there is just time. Thank you so much.'

Miss Grimbly bustled back. 'I must show you the geography. Tessa will have the guest-room, Paul must camp out on the settee. You naturally have no luggage – I will not inquire about those mysterious packages in blood-stained newspaper. But they seem to have aroused Rupert's interest, so they will be safer in my larder overnight.'

She made a pot of very weak tea. Goldilocks bombarded them with questions. For months she had seen no human being but Miss Grimbly. There had been so many long lonely days, so many cheerless nights in her dank hide-out. At last Miss Grimbly interrupted.

'Bedtime! I shall call you young people early, so that you can run home for breakfast. I am sorry I can spare you only a piece of bread to stay the pangs.'

It seemed all wrong that Goldilocks had to go through the camouflaged door and down the steps while Tessa retired like a lady to the guest-room and even Paul could curl up under a blanket on the settee. But even before Miss Grimbly had turned out the lights the wisdom of the precaution became obvious.

Rupert sat up, suddenly alert. He growled, then erupted into a series of staccato barks. Footsteps were clumping up the garden-path. Then came a peremptory knock. A voice shouted: 'Open! Police!'

'Quiet, Rupert,' said Miss Grimbly. She sailed into the hall, drew bolts, unfastened a chain. She returned with two Germans in the uniform of the Field Police. Their manner was now apologetic. In broken English they explained that they were searching for an escaped prisoner.

'We have seen nobody. You may look in all the rooms.'

They did so, poking under beds, peering into cupboards. 'And these children – they are yours, madam?'

'Certainly not! I am an unmarried lady! They are pupils from my school.'

'Of course! A thousand pardons, madam.'

Crestfallen, the Germans withdrew. For a few minutes they could be heard trampling about in the garden, investigating the tool-shed and summerhouse. But clearly the coal-house door was too cunningly screened for them to notice it. Soon their footsteps receded and the night was silent once more.

14

When you were a child, thought Tessa grimly, secrets
were fun. In reality they could be a burden, as now. But
she was hardly a child, she reminded herself. It was 1943,
almost three years since the Nazis came.

Naturally not a word must be breathed at school about
Goldilocks – though what news it would have been to
pass round! What most troubled her, though, was keeping the secret from her mother. There had never been
anything important that she could not share. Yet it had to
be done. There was quite enough rumpus at home over
the black-market meat. Her mother bore the brunt of
this.

'You must be mad!' cried Mr Gray. 'If one word leaked
out to the Germans! How often have I told you – '

Mrs Gray interrupted with unusual spirit. 'What
you've never told me is how to feed the family on the
rations! Four growing children – '

'I know – but you must think of my job, my pension – '

'At this rate we shan't live to draw your pension. *I* have
to think of the next meal.'

Tessa fled to her room. She hated to hear them quarrel-
ling. It happened more and more nowadays. It was the
same in many families. Paul's Gran blamed the Occupa-

tion for spoiling their childhood. Tessa was beginning to see what it could do to older people's personal relationships.

Even without her solemn promise to Miss Grimbly she could not have confided in her parents. For her father, as a public servant, the burden would have been intolerable.

It was easier for Paul. His father had made the hide-out and was already involved. He had a private word with Paul in his workshop. He smiled across the work-bench.

'Reckon you know something about Miss Grimbly's cottage now that I didn't mean you to know?'

'Yes, Dad.' Paul explained all that occurred.

'Can't be helped. Just keep it dark, that's all. Not a word to your mum. Or Lucy. Not fair to drag *them* in.'

'I wouldn't have told any one. But *you* knew.'

'One day we'll all have a good laugh about it.' Dad began to sort his tools, singing Vera Lynn's song under his breath, 'Tomorrow, just you wait and see.'

'Oh, you are lucky,' said Tessa when Paul told her. 'Being able to talk to your father like that!' When he protested that not another syllable had been spoken between them she looked at him as if he were stupid. 'It's the unspoken understanding,' she said grandly. 'You don't realise.'

Keeping the secret was only the beginning. '*Do* you realise, though, that they have to live on Miss Grimbly's single ration? It must be grim.'

They resolved to do what they could to help. Whenever they went out foraging for their own families they set a little aside for Miss Grimbly. A loaf, half a dozen potatoes, a few parsnips scrounged from a field . . . Miss

Grimbly accepted everything gratefully. No gift was more welcome than a tablet of toilet-soap from a damaged boxful Lucy had brought home from the shop.

At first these items were handed over at school. Then Copperknob, observing Tessa with a package which Miss Grimbly slipped into her desk, began dropping nasty remarks about 'Teacher's pet'. After that, Paul made the delivery on his weekly visit to the organ-loft, or occasionally he and Tessa would cycle up to the cottage. If the coast was clear they were able to see Goldilocks and tell her all the news.

'All the news' was a phrase that soon acquired a special significance.

Researching in the public library for their school essay they made a discovery. Few other people entered the quiet reference room while they were there, but at least half of them made a bee-line for a particular shelf, pulled out a dull-looking old volume, pored over it for some minutes, and went out again.

After this had happened the third time Tessa whispered: 'I wonder what's so interesting. It's the same book again.' Now that they were alone once more she ran across to the shelf. The mystery was solved as soon as she turned the pages. 'Come over here,' she said urgently.

She was looking at something she had heard of but never seen. A single sheet of thin paper, closely typed on both sides – that same day's issue of *GUNS*, *Guernsey Underground News Service*, published in defiance of the Nazis to spread the news they were constantly trying to falsify or suppress.

Nobody knew who edited *GUNS*, who typed out the

few dozen carbon copies, who passed them round. Milk-men, shopkeepers, all sorts of people helped in this risky work.

'*Our bombers attacked targets in Berlin last night*,' read Paul under his breath. Most of the news-sheet was compiled from BBC broadcasts the night before, but with a stop press summary of the eight o'clock bulletin that very morning. They scanned the typescript hastily, exclaiming with pleasure at any encouraging item, alert for any stranger coming into the room. They were able to replace the volume and return to their homework without being disturbed.

'It's a super idea,' said Paul. All radios were now banned. Though many people still had their hidden sets there were far more who had not. Everyone was hungry for news, and, now that it was getting better, with the war going against Hitler, it was understandable that the German commandant was doing everything in his power to keep people in ignorance.

The blitz on Britain had largely faded into a memory. It was the Germans now who, as this news-sheet reported, were being raided by the American and British bombers. The Allies had driven the enemy out of North Africa and were fighting their way up through Italy. Mussolini and his Fascists had been overthrown. In Russia the Red Army was advancing and reoccupying the vast Soviet territories lost to the Germans earlier in the war.

Best of all, Britain was becoming one vast armed camp as thousands and thousands of American troops crossed the Atlantic to build up an irresistible invasion force. One day soon, with the British themselves and the Canadians, the Free French and the other allies, they'd be coming over the Channel to set Europe free. And that would include the islands!

The Germans knew that. They must be shivering. Why else were they turning Guernsey into another Gibraltar? Why else bring over all these slave-labourers to tunnel the cliffs, mix concrete, carry stone until they dropped?

Though the war was going better, conditions in the island itself were harsher than ever. British people not born in Guernsey were being deported to France. Major Sherwill had been taken again, with a shipload of others. Sailing out of St Peter Port they had defied their guards by singing *There'll always be an England* for everyone ashore to hear.

Of course the news most hungrily sought was the personal news of families and friends in the outside world, especially those who had left Guernsey in the evacuation or even earlier to join the British forces. After the heartache of the first year's silence brief messages were filtering through via the International Red Cross.

Paul never forgot the expression on Dr McNish's face when he told them he'd at last had word from his wife: she was well, and so was their little daughter, now a year old. It was the first the doctor had heard of her existence.

Gran was both delighted and disgusted. 'What a thing, this war! Not to have seen your own child! Don't know how you can bear it.'

'There's many worse off,' said the doctor sadly.

Another winter was drawing to an end, to every one's relief. Coal was scarce as gold nuggets. There were electricity cuts and you were exhorted to save gas. Cooking – when you'd anything to cook – became a co-operative arrangement, neighbours sharing one oven.

Paul's services as organ-blower were more in demand than ever. Sometimes he helped out on Sundays, but he preferred the practice sessions when there was a chance to talk. 'I *like* old Grumbly,' he told Gran. 'She's an interesting old bird. Been to all sorts of places when she was young.'

'H'm,' said Gran. She disapproved of foreign travel, especially for ladies. And of boys calling their teachers old birds. 'Old bird, indeed! Birds are flighty.'

'Shouldn't wonder if *she* was – at one time.' He wished he could tell Gran what a spirit of adventure was still alive inside the genteel Miss Grimbly. He wondered if he would ever see as much of the world as Miss Grimbly had. Venice and Vienna and the Isles of Greece! Maybe, when he was grown up. This war couldn't last for ever.

One afternoon, as they came down from the organ-loft, they realised that once more, as in the old days, they had had an audience.

A shadow emerged from the shadows – that was the only way to describe it. Fischer was truly a shadow of the good-looking young officer they had known. Until he spoke they did not recognize him.

Outside in the daylight the shock was even greater. He was so thin. And so pale. Yet pale as he was, the scars stood out even whiter. He limped, and he never removed the leather glove from his right hand.

In her first pleasure Miss Grimbly – she who would never shake hands with her country's enemies – had made a gesture to do so, but even inside the church she had sensed her error just in time. Instead, she had turned the movement into a friendly pat on the arm.

'Are you posted back here?'

'Yes, Miss Grimbly, I have been very fortunate.' You could have fooled *me*, thought Paul. 'I was invalided home from the Eastern Front. It is good to hear your music again.'

'Was it – was it very terrible in Russia?' Paul asked.

'The weather was the worst.' Fischer laughed bitterly. 'The frostbite. I shall never play the piano again.'

'Dear God!' said Miss Grimbly hoarsely. Only now did Paul realise the full significance of the gloved hand. He stared at it with an irresistible fascination. How often had he exulted in the news of the Russian victories! It had been wonderful to think of Hitler being humiliated at Stalingrad and all those other strange-sounding places. Only Hitler himself hadn't been lying there, bleeding on the snow. Men like Fischer had.

After that, when he heard good news from the Eastern Front, he was still thankful, but thankful in another sense as well, that Fischer was no longer suffering there.

It was not long, however, before their secret source of news dried up. Three days running, Paul slipped into the reference library, only to find the same old copy of the news-sheet unchanged. On the fourth occasion it had gone. No later issue ever replaced it.

A rumour was going round the town. Most people had heard of *GUNS* even if they had never seen it.

Charles Machon, a printer on the *Guernsey Star*, had been arrested. So had the assistant editor, Mr Falla. Their regular helpers had been two carpenters and a greenhouse worker. One of these had been betrayed to the German police by an informer. All five were now awaiting trial.

'Daft,' said Slippery. 'What they thought they were gettin' out of it? Nobody payin' 'em anything!'

The Germans had found a typewriter at Mr Machon's house, concealed in a deep armchair.

'They took him away and beat him up cruel,' said Copperknob with gusto.

'Told him his old mother'd be sent off to Germany if he didn't talk. Now that was smart,' said Slippery.

Soon afterwards the five men were tried, sentenced to various terms of imprisonment, and sent to Germany.

'They asked for it,' said Slippery. 'You wouldn't catch *me* –'

'No,' said George Gasson, 'nobody would, would they?'

Slippery had no use for heroes. Other people had. Later, alone with Paul in the boys' wash-room, George propounded a startling idea. 'Some one's got to step into the gap,' he ended.

Paul had been quite carried away by his eloquence. 'Why not?' he said. 'The Jerries wouldn't suspect school-kids.'

'Are you on, then?'

'Sure,' said Paul. After that he could not go back.

15

Tessa of course had to know. And refused to be left out.

'It could be risky,' George warned her.

'Obviously. For you too.'

'There's your father,' said Paul.

'He won't know. Nor will yours. They'd stop us.'

The boys saw that they could not do without her. Only she could get the use of a typewriter.

How lucky Mr Gray had insisted on her joining the secretarial class! She had rebelled against his view that a girl's destiny was an office-job until she found a husband, but now she would be the kingpin – or rather the queenpin – of the enterprise.

The class had only four typewriters and much individual practice had to be fitted into lunch hours. Sometimes she would have the room to herself.

The three friends worked out the scheme on a long Saturday afternoon walk collecting firewood.

Mostly the boys would have to gather the news. Tessa had no chance to hear BBC bulletins at home. George had his own concealed crystal-set. Paul was limited in his listening. Dad kept things under strict control, switching on only when it seemed safe. But Paul had another source of information.

Goldilocks took Miss Grimbly's portable to her hide-out and was an avid listener throughout her long solitary days. She proved an invaluable collector of news. It was awkward that he could not tell even George that she was alive and helping them.

They could not hope to get out a daily issue. Twice a week was the most they could manage. With three typings on thin paper Tessa could produce fifteen legible copies. But how to circulate them?

One copy they could plant in the old book at the reference library – and watch if people discovered it. A few copies could be pushed anonymously into the letterboxes of sympathetic people likely to pass on their contents. Tessa would slip a copy into Uncle Percy's hand, pretending she had picked it up in the road.

'If only we could trust Slippery,' said Paul. But they all knew they couldn't. Slippery's flair for fixing things would have been so useful, but only a fool would have trusted him with such a secret.

They would have to be content with a small circulation. At least it would be whispered round that some one had taken over the job once performed by *GUNS*.

'We can demonstrate that Guernsey isn't beaten,' said George. 'Show that someone still has the guts – '

'Guts!' cried Tessa excitedly. 'How about that for a title? It was *GUNS* before — we could call ours *GUTS*.'

'What's the *T* stand for?' George demanded.

They racked their brains for a suitable word. In the end they settled for the *Guernsey Underground Temporary Service*. Temporary it was all too likely to be.

They launched the first issue a week later. It was quite a

111

job, selecting the items, cutting and compressing the words into two sides of single-spaced typing. They checked grammar and spelling with immense care, especially when there were tricky foreign names. They must remember that it was the 'Ruhr' valley we had bombed, though it sounded like 'roor', and that the Italian who came over the air as 'Chano' must be spelt 'Ciano'. The news-sheet must not betray that it was the work of people still at school.

Paul began to wonder if he might not like being a journalist when he grew up. He could understand the fascination of the work.

But how he wished he knew shorthand! Sometimes he had heard the same broadcast as George, but they had different recollections. George was against taking a lot of notes. He prided himself on his memory. Safer to carry things in your head.

'I shall take notes,' said Paul stubbornly, 'but don't worry, I'll use the Greek alphabet.'

He used an old rough notebook, so that his secret jottings were all mixed up with genuine schoolwork and doodles. The fair copies went to Tessa only on the day she was to type them.

They produced three issues of *GUTS* before the Easter holidays. Very soon Uncle Percy was taking Tessa aside with a twinkle in his eye. 'Seen anything more of interest lyin' about in the road?'

'You mean –'

'Never mind what I mean, my dear. Just remember, your uncle has a taste for readin'. So have several of his pals. Pals he can trust.'

After that, Tessa always 'happened to find' three copies of each issue. She slipped them to Uncle Percy while her mother's back was turned. He was as good as a conjuror at making things vanish.

The school holidays were frustrating. They could find no way to get access to a typewriter. There was nobody they could trust with their secret. As soon as the summer term began they rushed out a fresh issue.

Circulation was now twenty, total readership unknown. It meant four typings. Tessa sighed for the school duplicator, used for running off exam papers, but there was no chance to get access to it. Still, the drudgery was worth while. They were doing something to keep up public morale. It was thrilling when they heard people talking about their news-sheet and speculating about the identity of the 'men' behind it.

'It's going great guns,' said George exultantly.

Paul laughed. 'Great guts, you mean!'

'But we mustn't get above ourselves,' Tessa warned them. 'We can't afford to relax and get careless.'

The thought sobered them. Precautions could be boring but they had to be taken. No one must ever see what Tessa was typing. The extra consumption of paper and carbons must not be noticed. It was too dangerous to hoard used carbon sheets for another day, lest someone find them and decipher the impression of the previous typing. So they must be carefully destroyed at once.

Throughout May *GUTS* appeared regularly twice a week. The first June issue was ready for typing, word-lengths totalled so as not to overrun the space. Tessa had the handwritten sheets interleaved with an essay she did

113

not have to deliver until next week. Paul whispered to her:

'Some terrific bombing raids – heard this morning on the news. Sounded like softening up before the Allies start invading. If we cut two paragraphs of that stuff about Italy we could slip in a stop press – '

'Give it me then – '

'I've not had a chance to write it out. But I've got notes, I can dictate it to you – '

'O.K. See you in the typing room.'

They gobbled their scanty war-time lunch. He gave her a few minutes' start, then followed with the notebook rolled up in his blazer pocket. The dry clicketty-click of the keys met his ears as he reached the upstairs corridor. He peeped through the glass panel in the door. Tessa was alone, her back to the wall, so that no one could look over her shoulder. He walked in. 'Hiya!'

She paused. 'You've come just right. I'll finish this bit.'

'Fine.' He opened his notebook, thinking out a paragraph to summarise the exciting facts and figures he had heard and jotted down over breakfast.

'Right,' she said, fingers poised. 'Fire away.'

'Capitals, "*STOP PRESS*". Next line: "*Heavy bombing raids are reported on enemy communications throughout northern France, dislocating roads and railways. It is thought that the Allies are about to open the Second Front with landings on the Channel coast –* " '

It was not the Second Front that opened at that moment, but the door of the typing room. Mr Dexter entered. Behind him came two Germans in the uniform of the Field Police.

The headmaster looked sharply at Paul. 'What are *you* doing here? Boys have no business – '

It would have been comic if it had not been so serious. Here they were, producing an illegal news-sheet under the eyes of two Nazis, and all that was worrying old Dexter was finding a boy and girl alone in a classroom during the lunch-break.

'I – I'm sorry, sir – '

'Go along, then.'

One of the policemen broke in sharply. 'No, Herr Rektor, the boy had better stay.' The other German closed the door and set his back against it.

'Very well,' said the head. 'I still don't know what this is all about.'

'It is mere routine, Herr Rektor. All typewriters are to be checked.'

Paul moved slightly to mask Tessa, so that she would have a chance to hide the incriminating material. He heard, behind him, the rustle of paper being drawn from the machine. Then the policeman marched straight over and he was forced to stand aside.

'Permit me.' He helped himself to several blank sheets, then went round the other tables, uncovering each typewriter and tapping out a few words. He noted the make and number of each machine. Finally he came back to Tessa's table. She gathered up her satchel and let him take her seat.

'This is yours?' he asked her, holding out Paul's notebook, open as he had put it down.

'It's mine, sir,' said Paul quickly.

The policeman was frowning suspiciously at the page.

115

'These strange signs – what are they?'

'Greek, sir.' Paul licked his dry lips and prayed. 'My Greek homework.'

Mr Dexter let out an incredulous cry. Paul turned and cast him a look of wild appeal, then did something that no boy in the school had ever done before. He winked at Mr Dexter. The headmaster's eyebrows shot up, but as his jaw dropped he was momentarily unable to speak. He knew that Paul did not learn Greek. It was not taught in the school.

The policeman was fortunately still frowning at the notebook. 'This I shall take. Also I require a list of all children who use these machines.'

Just then there was a tap on the door, the other policeman stood aside, and Oberleutnant Fischer walked in. Seeing his rank, the other two Germans clicked heels, saluted and remained at attention.

'I am sorry, Headmaster,' said Fischer, 'but I was told you were here. May I ask what is happening?'

'The police have some idea that the school typewriters may have been used to produce an illegal newspaper.'

'Indeed?' Fischer turned to the man who still held the notebook. Paul's heart sank as he caught the meaning of his reply. These strange characters might be a code. The police had their orders – any suspicious writing, any language they could not understand, must be taken and shown to a higher authority.

'Excellent,' said Fischer approvingly. 'Most correct.' The man almost purred. 'But perhaps I can save you trouble. I studied Greek at my university in Heidelberg.' He took the notebook. Paul almost stopped breathing.

For an age Fischer studied his coded notes on bombed railway junctions and marshalling yards. Then, softly, he began to declaim long, rolling, musical lines of verse in an unknown tongue. It was Paul's turn to drop his jaw in amazement.

'This is ancient Greek,' Fischer assured the policeman. 'From Homer's great poem, the *Iliad*. Beautiful,' he added in English, handing the notebook back to Paul. 'Those very lines I learnt by heart myself.'

I'll bet you did, thought Paul, for you certainly didn't read them out of my notebook.

The policeman seemed satisfied. Tessa and Paul were allowed to go.

'Goodness,' she said outside, '*that* was a near one.'

'We're not out of the wood yet,' he said grimly.

The police still had their samples of typing from each school machine. It was only a matter of time before their experts identified the one used for *GUTS*.

'They still have to pin it on *you*,' said George. 'Lots of girls do typing. And any one else might sneak in. . . .'

They tried to be optimistic, but it wasn't easy. Luckily, by the next day, the Germans had bigger matters on their minds.

16

Tessa slept badly that night.

The day's alarms, and fears for the future, kept her awake or restlessly dreaming by fits and starts. Then she sat up, ears pricked to the droning in the sky.

She remembered – almost four years ago! – the early morning when the Germans were flying in. This sounded like something far bigger. The darkness vibrated with the incessant noise, swelling to an almost unbearable loudness overhead, then fading into the distance, then swelling again. Every few minutes, predictable as waves breaking on the beach.

Dry-mouthed, she longed for a drink. She poked her feet into her slippers and groped her way to the landing. Faint candle-light filtered up from the kitchen. She crept downstairs. 'It's only me,' she called softly.

Her parents were drinking the wishy-washy liquid that nowadays they pretended was tea. 'We couldn't sleep, either,' said her mother. She sounded very cheerful.

'What's happening?' Tessa hardly dared to hope.

'Please God, it's the Second Front. Those planes have been going over for hours.'

Tessa took a cup and drank thirstily. They talked in low voices. Upstairs the boys and little Shirley slept on.

After a while Mr Gray drew the curtains and opened the door to the fresh-scented dawn. He walked out on to the tiny lawn he had refused to dig up for vegetables. 'Listen,' he said. 'Naval guns! Over towards Cherbourg.'

'Then it's really happening!' Tessa ran out in her skimpy pyjamas, heedless of the dew that soaked her slippers. Her father was pointing upwards.

The pink and grey sky was speckled with troop-carriers moving southwards in formation. The gliders were towed in lines, like the tails of kites. It was awe-inspiring to think that up there were thousands of tense-faced soldiers, armed and helmeted, bound for the long-promised liberation of Europe. From the mainland came the continual grumble of massive guns.

Mrs Gray chivvied Tessa indoors. 'Get some clothes on. I know it's June, but you'll catch your death – '

Tessa had no intention of catching her death, today of all days. She ran upstairs. If only they had a wireless! But by the time she was dressed there had been a message from next door. Even the German radio was admitting Allied assaults on the Normandy coast. Then, as the Grays sat at breakfast, they heard through the open window their neighbours' radio turned up to full volume.

'Really!' cried her father. 'That's *most* unwise – '

But the children were already in the garden. Frank yelled: 'Quick! It's Eisenhower!'

It was indeed the voice of the American supreme commander, telling the peoples of Europe that D-day had come and liberation was on its way. Then other national leaders came one by one to the microphone, General de Gaulle speaking to the French, King Haakon to the

Norwegians, each to his own countrymen throughout the occupied continent. The words rolled out – Polish and Danish and Dutch too, incomprehensible but obvious in their significance. Victory! The end of the war!

Even Mr Gray had for once forgotten what time it was. Suddenly he looked at his watch, let out a cry of horror, and rushed away to his office. Tessa realised she'd be late for school. Would there *be* school? In any case she was eager to find her friends.

Outside, the first person she met was the sergeant-major. Hermann was festooned with equipment, his helmet fantastically wreathed in foliage. All the soldiers scurrying about were similarly in full battle order, with camouflage, as if expecting to see khaki-clad commandoes round the next corner. The townspeople were openly giving the forbidden V-sign. There was a general air of euphoria, almost intoxication.

School was crowded, though no one was doing any work. Staff and pupils were excitedly exchanging news.

Paul said that his father's telephone had gone dead. This seemed general. The Germans had put the exchange under armed guard. No calls were going through.

The Guernsey policemen were confined to their own station. They had obeyed German orders throughout the occupation, but at this moment of crisis the enemy were taking no chances. All defences were manned in case the Allies attempted a landing.

George's father thought they wouldn't – yet. With luck, the Nazis would get out of their own accord, rather than be caught in a trap.

Everybody was delighted that the Second Front had

been opened so near. The Allies had been expected to go for the shorter sea-crossing to the Calais area. They had outwitted Hitler by aiming for the Cherbourg peninsula, which meant that the Channel Islands would be among the very first places to be freed.

Never had there been such a diligent study of atlases. Geography had become the most popular school subject.

Mr Dexter begged every one to keep calm and not wander far from home. If there *were* an Allied landing there might be a lot of shooting. But like George's father he hoped they would be spared the terrible destruction of a battle for the island. 'The Germans will need every man to hold the mainland,' he said. 'They'll probably withdraw from here to reinforce their defences in France.'

Slippery liked the idea of this. 'If they do a bunk,' he said thoughtfully, 'they'll have to leave a lot of stuff behind them. Enemy property.... And somebody'll have to do a bit of clearing up after 'em.' He sounded more than ready to help in this patriotic task.

But there was no sign of the Germans departing that day. At supper Mr Gray said, 'Better not count our chickens too soon.' He was right. The BBC said that the Allies had established a bridgehead and that men, tanks and guns were pouring ashore. This was only on the French coast, however – here in Guernsey the Nazis manned their defences for an attack that never came.

Days passed, then weeks. The news was splendid – for everyone else. The fortified Atlantic Wall of the Nazis was shattered, the Allies were fanning out over Normandy, Churchill had been over to see their progress, so had the King....

There was no need for a secret newspaper now. The Germans had ceased to bother about illegal radios – many of them, distrusting their own propaganda bulletins, openly asked the islanders what the BBC was saying.

Outwardly, nothing had changed. The swastika flags still floated over St Peter Port. 'I reckon,' said Gran dourly, 'those people in London have clean forgot about *us*.'

17

No one would have thought it possible. After D-Day, life in the island grew worse.

Not a German soldier left. Only the slave labourers were shipped off to France while it was still possible. Hitler had given orders to defend the Channel Islands to the last. The Nazis wanted no extra mouths to feed.

'They'll be sending *us* away, next,' said Paul's mother gloomily. But that fear was soon removed. Once the Allied troops had broken out of the Cherbourg peninsula, some swung westwards and overran Brittany while others pushed east towards Paris. The Guernsey garrison could not escape to the mainland even if it wanted to, and neither could it deport unwanted civilians.

The Germans were cut off from their own supply-lines. It was a stark new situation for everybody. Until now, though cut off from Britain for four years, the island had received food from France. Now the blockade was complete, both ways.

Running to find her father in the garden, Tessa could not believe her eyes. 'What *are* you doing?'

He paused in his digging. 'You can see.'

'But the *lawn*! Your beautiful lawn!'

He grunted, and drove his spade savagely into the turf.

Ever since she could remember, that lawn had been sacred. No rough play must blemish it. It had been mown and rolled, watered and dressed, swept of leaves and worm-casts. Now the loving work of years was being sacrificed in an hour.

She had often laughed at Father's obsession. She was older now, had grown in imagination as well as body. Compassion almost choked her. 'We're going to be hungry before this war is over,' he said.

Already his beloved border, his dahlias and chrysanthemums, had gone to make room for rows of potatoes and beans. Now the lawn, once smooth as a snooker-table, was a lumpy expanse of brown clods. He dug deep and ferociously, as if to bury an enemy.

'I can plant winter spinach and spring cabbage,' he said, 'onions maybe, autumn and winter lettuce....' Luckily there was already a good crop of potatoes – *they* were the standby. Some people were thankful to eat potatoes one day and the peelings the next, made into a sort of pie. 'We're all turning into vegetarians,' Mr Gray panted. They usually had soup for the midday meal, using what vegetables they had. Breakfast now was a single slice of bread.

Tessa was always hungry. When school started again in the autumn she felt limp and tired. She found it hard to concentrate on the work in the new class, though moving up was something she'd always looked forward to.

'I get muddled,' she told Paul. 'I can't remember things.'

Copperknob chipped in. '*I* can't either, Tess.'

'You never could,' she said contemptuously, then felt

bad about it. Her temper now was shorter. That was another thing.

She'd study herself in her bedroom mirror. She was so *flat*. A girl wanted to be slim, but not thin. She overheard Dr McNish reassuring her mother. 'Don't worry. She'll soon fill out when the food situation gets easier.'

Food was the constant topic at school. The girls talked wistfully of feasts and parties long ago. 'You can feel my bones,' said Tessa mournfully.

'Thanks,' said Slippery, who had crept up on them.

'I said my *bones*!' she cried furiously, and slapped his face as she struggled free. It was a feeble blow – she had no strength for anything nowadays – and Slippery merely grinned.

'You don't look half bad when you go red.'

That was another maddening thing. She was so pale now, positively anaemic. It took this lout's groping paw to bring colour to her cheeks.

Slippery showed no sign of under-nourishment. He was one of the biggest boys in the school. He looked after himself, he always said.

'Bet you do!' said George.

'I mean exercises an' all that.'

Nobody had spare energy for exercises. The school had cut down on strenuous games and physical training. Slippery looked well because he got more to eat. How he got it was anybody's guess. There was a lot of petty thieving, not just from the enemy but from fellow-islanders, as hunger made people desperate. Nothing, however, could ever be pinned on Slippery.

Paul and Tessa worried often about Miss Grimbly and

Goldilocks, eking out one ration between them. It was increasingly hard to get Miss Grimbly to accept anything. 'You must not rob your own families,' she said. 'Your duty is to them.'

She accepted a few potatoes from the Grays' garden, a bag of sawdust and wood scraps from Mr Le Grand's workshop, but otherwise she would take only a little of what they could gather in the fields and lanes for their mothers – blackberries and mushrooms, acorns and firewood. It wasn't easy to find anything, with so many other people out on the same quest.

What a mercy, thought Paul, that poor old Jenny had died – of old age – last spring. Even Miss Grimbly had shed tears when she had braced herself to take Rupert to the vet. It was only kindness, she explained. This was no world for a healthy spaniel. He had lived happily; she would not watch him starve to death.

There were hardly any pets left in the island, and they had to be guarded or they disappeared. The German soldiers were ravenous too. They snared rabbits when they could, but it was hard to find rabbits now.

Early in December came a rumour. The Red Cross was going to send in food parcels like those they were allowed to send to prisoners-of-war. 'I should think so,' said Gran. '*We're* prisoners of war.'

'How wonderful,' said Lucy, 'if they came by Christmas!'

A BBC broadcast encouraged their hopes. A neutral ship was sailing from Lisbon, and the Royal Navy would let it through if the Germans promised that all parcels would be given to the civilians.

126

Christmas brought only disappointment. ' "Saw three ships come sailing in"!' Paul quoted bitterly. 'I'd be glad to see *one*, never mind three.' No one had much heart for carol-singing. An extra slice of bread each was the extent of their celebrations.

But two days later he was shouting down from his bedroom window. A ship was steaming into the port. There were huge red crosses painted on her sides.

The *Vega* had arrived, an old Swedish vessel with a tall thin funnel trailing filthy smoke. But a gilded treasure galleon would not have been so beautiful. He raced down to the harbour. He found Tessa there, and half the town.

Now there were days of tantalising suspense. The Red Cross officials had to confer with the Germans. The Germans would unload the parcels but Guernsey representatives would supervise to ensure that none fell into the wrong hands. After that, the parcels were stored under lock and key. Finally they were distributed to the various shops where people were registered for their rations. On the Sunday, the last day of 1944, the parcels could be collected.

Miss Grimbly was house-bound, recovering from a bad chill. Tessa and Paul carried her parcel up to her cottage. It was a wonderful moment.

'Rosa! Come quickly!' cried Miss Grimbly, swinging back the camouflaged door. Goldilocks' footsteps could be heard, not running, but stumbling a little. Her face was grey, the stretched skin papery, but she managed her old smile for them.

'It has come,' declaimed Miss Grimbly. 'It has really come. From the Canadian Red Cross!'

127

'Some of the parcels were from New Zealand,' said Paul, anxious to be fair.

'We will not argue about geography.' She tore at the wrappings. 'Coffee!' she cried.

'There's tea too,' said Paul.

'And cocoa,' said Tessa.

One by one the items were pulled out, brandished exultantly, set out in display on the table. There were sardines, tinned salmon, flour, biscuits, sugar, corned beef, dried fruits –

'We can have a belated Christmas pudding,' announced Miss Grimbly. 'Butter, cheese, dried milk, condensed milk, chocolate, pork products – whatever *they* are – '

'Lovely to think,' said Tessa, 'there's a parcel for every family in the island.'

'We must celebrate,' Miss Grimbly decided. 'I shall make a pot of tea – real tea. We'll open the biscuits.'

And in tea, real tea, they drank to the unknown friends who had sent the parcels – and to victory and liberation in the New Year.

18

'I reckon those parcels just about saved our lives,' said Gran, and it was simple truth.

Tessa had walked in to find her sitting up as usual in bed, wispy white hair straggling from under the headphones of the crystal-set Paul had made for her.

The Germans no longer bothered about illegal radios. Tessa's father no longer bothered about her friendship with Paul. There was a limit nowadays to what any one could bother about. So Tessa often came in and Gran specially enjoyed her visits. The mittens Gran was wearing had been a Christmas present from Tessa, knitted from precious wool unpicked from an old cardigan.

Gran mostly stayed in bed. It was the only warm place.

There had been no gas supply since Christmas. Electricity was cut off during the night. Even at the hospital only a serious emergency justified the lighting of its hoarded candles. The main water was turned on for only three hours each day. So cooking was difficult and a fire was a rare luxury.

It was useless to scour the lanes for wood. The Germans, desperate as anyone, were felling all trees and sawing them up for fuel. Mr Le Grand's workshop still had some sawdust and waste scraps of wood. Paul took a bagful to the Grays. Mr Gray sent some home-grown potatoes in return.

He eyed Paul with cautious approval, asking him questions about school. With the Allied armies sweeping across Europe it was becoming possible to talk – fingers crossed – about the future.

'You'll join your father when you leave?'

'I'm not sure I'd be good enough.'

Mr Gray's eyebrows rose. 'Good enough?'

'Dad's taught me a lot – but I'm not that good with tools. *He*'s a real craftsman, every one says. I'd hate to let him down.'

'H'm. . . . What would you like to be?'

'I – I think I'd *like* to be a journalist.' Paul felt himself going red.

'A journalist! Whatever put that into your head?'

How could he explain? Mr Gray mustn't know about the secret news-sheet. Fortunately he was eager to express his own views and did not wait for an answer. 'I like a lad with ambition,' he said generously. 'But – *journalism*! Not much security. Still, if I can ever help – a word to the editor of the *Star* – '

'That's really good of you, Mr Gray. I'll remember.'

He couldn't say that actually his dreams were of Fleet Street, perhaps even of roving the wide world as a special correspondent. The wide world. . . . That's what he was dreaming of, now that there was a chink of daylight opening between the prison gates.

He had pinned up an old map of Europe in his bedroom. The colours and boundaries were all wrong, of course. Pre-war. But the rivers and cities were the same.

With tiny home-made flags he marked the Allied advances.

The Russians had swept across the Polish plain into Hungary and into Germany itself. In the west France was free. The Americans and British and Canadians – all the western Allies in fact – were advancing again. By March Montgomery's forces were across the Rhine.

Why couldn't Hitler see that he was beaten? People kept saying, it's only a matter of time. But, said Mum despondently, so was starving to death. A Red Cross parcel wouldn't last for ever, though she doled out its contents crumb by crumb.

Why didn't the Germans in Guernsey, at least, acknowledge that their situation was hopeless? They too were starving. Even Hermann had lost his swagger. His uniform hung loose. He looked like a slowly deflating balloon.

'They won't surrender,' said Mr Gray. 'They've been ordered to hold out till the end. I'm afraid they will. One must admit, they're brave – and they're disciplined.'

If anything, their determination had stiffened. There was a new commander, Admiral Hüffmeier, a fanatical Nazi. He had just issued a proclamation to his men: '*I have only one aim: to hold out until final victory. I believe in the mission of our Führer and of our people. Heil our beloved Führer!*'

'Final victory!' echoed Mr Gray in disgust. 'The man's mad. Mad as Hitler himself. Think what it means!'

No one liked to think what it meant. Guernsey had become a fortress, the cliffs honeycombed with deep-set gun-emplacements. If the Allies had to storm it, how many defenceless civilians would survive? It was becoming a question of whether one would be blown to bits or would fade away slowly through famine.

Spirits soared when, after a month, the *Vega* sailed in with a second cargo. She returned after another month, bringing also malt and codliver oil for the schools, and flour so that the bakers could make bread again. The last issue of coarse brown bread had been on the twelfth of February. On the eighth of March the Grays sat down to a white loaf such as they had not seen for years.

Shirley was too young to remember at all. 'It's *gorgeous*!' she said.

'It's like cake,' said Harold.

Shirley couldn't remember cake either.

The Germans were still 'correct'. They did not take the Red Cross parcels for themselves. A few soldiers stole from houses, but some islanders did the same.

'I saw a soldier going through our dust-bin,' Harold reported. 'He pulled out that tin we'd had with the sardines in. It was *mucky*, but he wiped it round with his finger, and then sucked his finger – '

'Ugh!' said Shirley.

'He wouldn't have found much,' said their mother grimly. 'I've no sympathy for the Jerries. They should never have come here.'

How bitter Mother has grown, thought Tessa sadly, not sweet as she used to be. Understandable, though. It was specially hard for mothers, struggling to keep the home going, seeing their children with sunken eyes and matchstick legs. It wasn't just the hunger – it was the cold and the dark, the wearing out of clothes, the perpetual

132

problem of keeping clean without soap or enough hot water. The boys were for ever getting cuts and grazes that festered horribly and would not heal.

Schooling was disrupted, teachers too weak and ill to teach, children unable to concentrate. Gran was always complaining about her memory. 'Sign of old age,' she growled. Paul tried to console her, vowing that he had the same problem.

The *Vega* was supposed to come once a month. No one knew an exact date, but hopeful rumours flew around. Paul crossed off days on a home-made calendar. By the third week few families had much of their Red Cross parcel left.

Slippery came up to Tessa in the corridor. 'Like some chocolate?'

'That supposed to be funny?' she said. The very word 'chocolate' triggered off unbearable longings.

'No, honest, I got some. Milk, with nuts an' raisins.'

'Pinched, I s'pose?'

'Whatcher take me for?' He was the picture of scandalized virtue. 'Fair exchange it was.'

She longed to believe him.

'Course, if you're not interested,' he said.

'I am,' she said helplessly. 'Who wouldn't be?'

He glanced right and left along the corridor. It was Slippery's characteristic action, like road-safety kerb-drill. 'Not here, Tess. They'll be round us like bees. Only got the one bar to spare.'

One *bar*! A whole *bar*! She'd take it home, there'd be a bite for every member of the family. Temptation washed away all doubts. 'What about the library?'

Slippery looked reluctant. His mere appearance among the bookcases would rouse suspicious comment. 'Typin' room would be safer,' he said.

'O.K.' She slipped upstairs and after a moment he followed. He closed the door behind him and held out the promised bar of chocolate.

'I must pay for it,' she said. He would expect it. Dealing was his way of life. Nothing for nothing was his motto. But he said, 'No, Tess. What's a bar of choc between friends?'

'I'd sooner. Really.' She fingered the coins. She didn't want to take favours from him of all people. 'I must give you something.'

'Oh well . . . if you *insist*.' He came across the room. She'd never seen him with this sort of smile. She moved so that a table was between them. 'Fair exchange,' he murmured. 'An' no need to be coy – you're a big girl now.'

What a fool she'd been, she told herself in panic. She'd heard enough about him from the other girls.

He'd put away the chocolate. To leave his hands free. Slippery, who prided himself on his poker face, was looking pink and excited. She must get to the door. But, as she darted round the table, they collided and his clutching arms fastened round her.

'Let me go! You're hurting – '

'Take it easy,' he pleaded. 'Be your age.'

She heard the door open, but, squashed against his chest, she could not see who had come in. Nor did she much care. Even if it was Mr Dexter.

'Leave her alone!' It was Paul's voice. Slippery's

unwelcome embrace relaxed. He spun round. She clutched at the table to regain her balance.

'Keep your nose out of this – ' began Slippery. Before he could utter more his own nose received the full impact of Paul's fist. The boys grappled and rocked. Paul went down, Slippery straddling him. Enraged, Slippery seized Paul's head and began to bang it on the boarded floor.

She saw it was time to take a hand. Better still, an ear. Best of all, two ears. They belonged to Slippery, but after a few moments of Tessa's enthusiastic treatment he must have wondered how long he would retain them.

'You little bitch!' he howled.

'Get off him then!'

'*You* get off *me*!'

Fair enough. Slippery had released Paul's head but neither boy could rise until she got off Slippery's back. She dismounted and stood aside. The boys scrambled to their feet. Paul was fighting mad. She had never seen *him* look like this either. It was a day of discoveries.

Slippery edged towards the door. 'There was no need for all that,' he said in an injured tone. Slippery was not by nature a fighter. He preferred negotiation.

'Then don't you dare lay a finger on Tessa again!'

'She's not *your* girl, is she?'

'Yes, she is,' said Paul.

Tessa could have hugged herself. But she would sooner have hugged Paul.

The bell rang downstairs. Slippery went. They followed more slowly. 'Are you hurt?' she said.

'No! Take more than Slippery.'

'Thank God you came in – '

'Lucky I just saw him sneaking after you.'

She explained about the chocolate, admitting that she'd been absurdly innocent. 'I didn't encourage him, honest.'

Paul understood. In these days the mere thought of chocolate might unbalance any one's mental processes.

'I thought you were terrific,' she told him, 'when you bonked him on the nose like that – '

He did not confess that this too had been lucky. All his strength had gone into that first infuriated blow. When Slippery got him down on the floor he'd been scared. Slippery was going to knock hell out of him. He'd felt weak as a kitten – he always did, now. But Tess had plunged in to the rescue, and then, what with bluff and Slippery's own disinclination for a fight, he'd got away with it. If Tess had decided he was a hero, better not contradict her.

But it was humiliating to feel so weak. He still blew the organ for Miss Grimbly, Sundays as well, but nowadays the effort of working that wooden handle exhausted him.

Most churches gave up music that winter. There was no electric light, let alone power for the organs. Candles were unobtainable. People could not see their hymn-books. But Miss Grimbly carried on. 'Choose old favourites,' she instructed the Vicar, 'hymns they know by heart.'

At the end of April came the news that Mussolini had been caught by Italian partisans and shot. Meanwhile, the Red Army was fighting its way into Berlin itself. On the first of May came the greatest news of all – Hitler was dead, and it wasn't just the BBC saying so, it was given out on the Hamburg radio.

Admiral Hüffmeier decreed official mourning throughout the island, but even the German soldiers displayed little sign of grief, and every one else was celebrating joyfully, even in sight of the Nazis. To crown everything, the *Vega* steamed in with another cargo of food parcels. Hüffmeier ordered her captain to fly a flag at half mast while in harbour, but as a neutral he refused, and the Admiral could do nothing about it.

What a week it was! On Tuesday Berlin surrendered to the Russians, on Wednesday Hamburg gave in to the British, and by Friday Montgomery had received the surrender of all enemy forces in North-west Germany, Holland and Denmark. On other fronts the American generals were thrusting into the heart of the German homeland.

By Sunday the forbidden Union Jacks were fluttering all over Guernsey like spring flowers. After morning service Miss Grimbly played *Land of Hope and Glory* – and the congregation almost sang their heads off.

Outside in the May sunshine Fischer stepped forward and saluted. 'Miss Grimbly, may I speak? Or will it embarrass you?'

'Why should it embarrass me?'

'To be seen talking to a German at this time.'

'Nonsense, my dear man! Speak on.'

'Things are moving so fast, there may be no other chance to say thank you – and goodbye. With Hitler dead, even Admiral Hüffmeier will hardly try to hold Guernsey. Very soon all you good people will be free once more. But I, if I am still alive, will be a prisoner. And so. . . .' He shrugged.

'You will not be a prisoner for ever,' said Miss Grimbly bracingly. 'Doubtless many will have to be punished for their wickedness. I will be frank – I hope so. But *you* have been as much a victim as we have. No one will want to keep millions of Germans in prison. You *will* be free again.' She took a card from her handbag. 'This is my address. Write when you are able. We *must* know how you get on. Meanwhile, I shall pray for you.'

Fischer had been wise to take that chance to say goodbye. By the next day the war in Europe was as good as over: General Eisenhower had received the surrender of all German forces. On Tuesday the word ran round that Churchill would be broadcasting at three o'clock. Every hidden valve set was brought out and placed outdoors or by an open window, so that the Prime Minister's voice could be heard in every street.

'Hostilities end officially at one minute after midnight, but in the interests of saving life the "Cease fire" began yesterday to be sounded all along the front. . . .' And then followed, for Paul and Tessa and all the others listening, the electrifying words: 'And our dear Channel Islands are also to be freed today!'

19

'Today', Churchill had said. But as the long May evening passed without anything happening it looked as though it would be 'tomorrow'.

'Not to worry,' said Uncle Percy, quietly materialising in the Grays' kitchen. Uncle Percy should by rights have been in prison. The Germans had caught up with him at last for some minor breach of regulations and he'd been sentenced to three months. He'd been out after a couple of weeks. The Germans had more minor offenders than they had room for. Men were queueing up to serve their sentences. The authorities were so short of food that they sent them home.

'Not to worry,' Uncle Percy repeated, 'I just heard, it's this loony Hüffmeier being awkward to the last.'

Two Royal Navy destroyers were lying four miles off shore. Some German officers had been out to them. Hüffmeier didn't want to 'surrender', he demanded an 'armistice'. Hadn't he a whole division under his command, twenty thousand troops? He could not surrender to two small warships.

Uncle Percy chuckled. 'The officers were sent back with a flea in their ear! The British brigadier told 'em it was unconditional surrender – or else. Mark my words, our lads'll be here first thing in the morning.'

As usual Uncle Percy was right.

Paul saw them first. He woke, blinked into the sunrise, and there, besides the familiar sprawl of the island of Herm, two smaller shapes were silhouetted. The destroyers were coming in.

He rushed across to Lucy's room and banged on her door. 'They're here!' In moments his sister was beside him, barefoot, at his window. They drank in the vision, then ran down to Gran.

She was awake but had not drawn her curtains. Lucy helped her to sit up. 'Of course they've come!' cried Gran. 'I told you I'd see these Nazis out, and so I will.' She waved a blue-veined hand in greeting to the unseeing sailors still a mile outside the harbour. Then she surveyed Lucy. 'And *you'd* best make yourself decent, my girl. Victory or no victory, you can't go capering about in *that* skimpy thing.'

Luckily they had collected their Red Cross parcel only a few days before. They could celebrate with a pot of really strong tea and demolish a whole packet of biscuits with wild extravagance. The whole family gathered in Gran's room, so as not to lose sight of the destroyers. Then Paul went running down to Tessa's.

All the town was making for the waterfront. The harbour itself was shut off behind high barbed-wire gates, as it had been throughout the occupation, but they were able to worm their way forward to a good viewpoint near the Weighbridge. They let Shirley stand in front, with Frank and Harold, so that they could get a glimpse of the ships and their fluttering White Ensigns.

A German soldier was climbing up a tall dockside crane. They watched him mounting against the dazzling blue sky, a bundle slung over his shoulder. Then suddenly a great Union Jack opened like a flower, and the multitude below burst into a delirious cheer.

'Can't *we* have a flag?' Frank pleaded.

Tessa laughed. 'Well, you can't have that one.'

'No. But that boy over there is selling them.'

She turned. The boy, needless to say, was Slippery.

'Where'd you get *them*?' George Gasson asked as he pushed his way forward to join his friends. 'Lifted 'em, I bet!'

'I'll do you for slander one o' these fine days.' Slippery explained that he had got the little Union Jacks from Mrs Simkins, whose late husband had kept the fancy goods shop before the war. When it closed, she'd sold the other stock easily enough, but she'd had to hide the forbidden flags, not knowing what to do with them. Slippery *had* known.

Even today Tessa could not bring herself to buy one from him.

'Please yourself,' he said airily, 'if you don't *want* to be patriotic.' He moved on, doing a brisk trade.

Shirley set up a wail. 'Oh, *Tess*, why can't we?'

Luckily at that moment there was a diversion. The first British soldiers were streaming ashore and forming up on the quay. Bayonets flashed. And now they were actually coming! The barbed-wire gates swung back. Policemen tried vainly to hold back the crowd.

Once the khaki column emerged it was impossible to keep any sort of order. The ranks dissolved as people pressed forward with outstretched arms. The soldiers were hugged and kissed, and slanting rifles wavered crazily like grasses in a gale. The men stumbled rather than marched, their grinning faces patterned with the last of the lipstick the girls had hoarded for this day.

In return the men fumbled in their pockets, handing out chocolate and cigarettes. Shirley was given an orange. She looked mystified, having no memory of such a thing. She tried to bounce it on the flagstones.

'It's not a ball, silly,' said Frank. 'You eat it.'

'But you peel it first,' said Tessa quickly, as Shirley tried to sink her teeth in the fruit and looked frustrated.

They joined the surge of people accompanying the column along the Esplanade. They saw the Union Jack hoisted over the Royal Hotel that had so long been the German headquarters. And so the long joyous day unrolled, hour after hour, with cheers and tears, singing and dancing in the streets until long after dark.

Over the next few days they must have stood for hours, watching more arrivals. Minesweepers and troopships followed the destroyers. There were American tank-landing craft which let down drawbridges and disgorged not tanks but vast stores of food and other essential supplies. There were the fantastic amphibious DUKWS – 'ducks' indeed, and another American invention – that sailed into harbour but, instead of mooring at the Albert Pier, headed for the slipway and astounded the bystanders by driving straight up into the town, clanking and dripping as they came.

There was the joy of watching their liberators arrive, the unspeakable relief of seeing their enemies leave.

Admiral Hüffmeier himself, grey-faced and tight-lipped . . . then, in batch after batch, the columns of pallid soldiers, shabby and strange-looking without their helmets and equipment, marching down to embark in the vessels that would carry them into captivity.

One day they saw Hermann, more deflated than ever, and Paul hummed softly to himself, '*Kiss me good-night, Sergeant-major.*' People booed, and some of the German soldiers did not hide their smiles.

On the next day Paul and Tessa met Miss Grimbly in the town. With her was Goldilocks, free at last to come out into the world. Already there was more colour, even the first gilding of sunburn, in her cheeks. As they stood happily chattering another sad column of prisoners came marching down towards the harbour. Among them, head high, back straight, struggling to overcome his limp, was Kurt Fischer.

Recognition was instant. The young officer stared incredulously at Goldilocks. For a moment he seemed about to break ranks, but his military training checked the impulse. He marched on.

Paul could not bear him to go to his prison-camp without being sure that Goldilocks was really alive. He ran along the pavement, drew level with Fischer, and called out, 'It *is* Goldilocks – you know, sir, Miss Goldsmith – she didn't die – '

Fischer answered from the corner of his mouth. 'Thank God! Give her my . . . good wishes. Paul, tell her – I thank God.'

'Good luck yourself, sir!'

Some of the bystanders had begun to jeer. A boy

stepped forward and spat. Fischer wiped his cheek with his remaining hand. He marched on.

Paul saw that the boy was Slippery. He saw too that Miss Grimbly was panting at his side, her eyes ablaze. Slippery saw her too and vanished deftly into the crowd.

The blaze in Miss Grimbly's eyes had changed to a mistiness. 'I wish I could have caught up with Mr Fischer. I wanted to tell him, it is not the man we hate, only the uniform. Sometimes,' she went on fiercely, 'I detest *all* uniforms. But I remind myself, how thankful I was to see khaki again.'

Paul rejoined Tessa. They wandered on together.

'I wonder what will happen to Fischer,' he said, 'in the end.'

'I wonder what will happen to all of us. In the end.'

They knew no answer. From a window overhead a loudspeaker was blaring out the vibrant confident voice of Vera Lynn:

'Tomorrow – just you wait and see!'

Geoffrey Trease
A Flight of Angels £2.99

'Rodney was playing his torch beam further round the side of the cave. Suddenly the fold flashed back at him.'

Four children find that their history project provides more adventure and thrills than they thought possible, as they explore the sandstone caves underneath the city of Nottingham.

Geoffrey Trease
Aunt Augusta's Elephant £2.99

Clearing out their great-aunt's flat in Bath, Nicola and Tim discover
an amazing enamel egg, wrapped in a yellowing scarf.

It's the most beautiful thing they have ever seen.

But they don't know then how much trouble the egg is going to
cause – nor how it would change their lives for ever . . .

Sarita Kendall
Ransom For A River Dolphin £2.99

For the people who live along the River Amazon, dolphins are
magical animals . . .

When Carmenza finds a badly injured dolphin, she remembers the
harpoon her step-father lost on his last fishing trip. She knows he
doesn't understand the dangers of using a dolphin's tooth as a lucky
charm . . .

Hidden among the trees at the edge of the lake, the beautiful pink
dolphin is nursed back to health by Carmenza and her classmate
Ramiro.

But it is only Ramiro's father, a wise old Indian, who can divert the
anger of the wounded dolphin's spirit . . .

Nat Hentoff
This School is Driving Me Crazy £2.99

'Sometimes I think I am going crazy'

Scatty Sam has problems. How can he manage to get on at school when teachers expect him to be a whizz-kid – just because his father is headmaster!

In his efforts to survive in a rough and sometimes violent school, Sam ends up having to oppose his father and face expulsion. He knows that a gang of bullies are threatening the younger kids, but Sam is willing to be accused rather than tell.

Sam's story is continued in *Does This School Have Capital Punishment?*

also available in Piper.

Mary Wesley
Haphazard House £2.99

Haphazard House has been empty for years. A place of mystery,
damaged by fire and lost in time.

Then Lisa and her family arrive, falling for its crooked ways and
finding that the house more than lives up to its name.

Why does the village seem locked in the past? What is the secret of
the invisible gardener, and who is the eerie figure that waves from
the window of a room burnt long ago?

Rumer Godden
Mr McFadden's Hallowe'en £2.99

Hallowe'en is a special time in Scotland. Boys and girls dress up as ghosts, witches, bats and black cats and go visiting round the houses.

'I will be a good witch,' said Selina.

'There's no such thing,' said her sister Muffet.

But there was, and she brought good luck with her – to the village, to poor young Tim, but especially to Mr McFadden, the cross, friendless old farmer.

This was certainly one Hallowe'en *he* would never forget.

Douglas Hill
Galactic Warlord £2.25

He stands alone . . . his planet, Moros, destroyed by unknown forces. His one vow – to wreak a terrible vengeance on the sinister enemy.

But Keill Randor, the LAST LEGIONARY, cannot conceive the evil force he will unleash in his crusade against the WARLORD, the master of destruction, and his murderous army, the DEATHWING.

Deathwing Over Veynaa £2.25

The robot's attack proved one thing . . . that the Deathwing was on Veynaa – with a weapon that could destroy a world!

Only a small rebellion in a minor solar system but it was part of the evil master-plan of the mysterious GALACTIC WARLORD. And it would need all the special skills and courage of Keill Randor, the Last Legionary, and his alien companion Gir, to defeat the Warlord's agents, the Deathwing, and save the planet Veynaa.

Mary Wesley
The Sixth Seal   £3.50

Pink and green snowfalls in July are just the first in a series of disturbing incidents worldwide – until a deadly storm blasts the life out of everything it touches.

Only a few people remain, like Muriel, her son, Paul and his friend Henry, who are below ground when the storm strikes. Stranded in the Devon countryside, they band together with other survivors to make the most of their strange new world.

Inevitably, tensions rise and Henry leaves for London – and a bizarre confrontation in the Cabinet room of 10 Downing Street. Muriel and Paul set off in pursuit – and find themselves at the mercy of a nightmare city . . .